One Winter Night

An Echo Ridge Romance

Other Works by Heather

The DiCarlo Brides
A Perfect Fit
SEALed with Love
Reclaiming his Bride
Family Matters
Wild Hearts
The Last Bride
Getting Her Groom

Other books set in Juniper Ridge, Colorado
Homecoming

Carver Ranch Romances
Second Chances
Identity
Safe Haven

In The Garden Series
Hello Again
First Crush
Not in the Plans—coming soon
Last Chance—coming soon

Echo Ridge Anthologies
Christmas Kisses—One Winter Night
Kisses Between the Lines—Much Ado About a Kiss
Silver Screen Kisses— You've Got Email, coming March 2017

Other titles
Waypoint
Caribbean Hideaway—coming 2017
Dancing at the Flea Market
A Timeless Romance Anthology: Valentine's Day Collection—Deal Breaker

One Winter Night

An Echo Ridge Romance

Heather Tullis

Published by Jelly Bean Press, PO Box 548, Osawatomie, KS
66064
ISBN-10: 1-63034-042-1
ISBN-13:978-1-63034-042-1

Dedication

For Kindra—sometimes you have to go for your dreams,
even when nothing is going your way.
I'm so proud of you!

Chapter One

JONAH OWEN SMILED AT MRS. CHESTER, the prospective buyer for his grandmother's house. He saw the dispassionate way she studied the layout, the slight disdain in the lines of her mouth when she looked at the wheelchair lift in the bedroom, and the sneer that overcame her features when she gazed out the back window and focused on the next-door neighbor's house. "How many horses do they have?"

"Three or four I think. I'm not sure. She's very conscientious about cleaning up after them and the other animals." His grandmother had talked incessantly about her neighbor, Kaya's, animal therapy business, but he'd only met her briefly once or twice over the years. When the prospective buyer turned and looked at him with disbelief, he realized he'd said the wrong thing.

Mrs. Chester—the only name she'd offered him—narrowed her dark eyes at him. "*What* other animals? All I see are horses. How did she get zoned for *farm animals* anyway? I thought this was a residential zone."

"I believe she has a couple of goats, some chickens and maybe some rabbits. I'm not sure exactly. She does animal therapy with children, so she rarely has more than one other car over there at a time." He didn't really know as he hadn't spent much time at the house since he'd moved back to town. "Her family used to own all of this land once, for the entire subdivision, plus the Fieldstone Manor subdivision. Since they've had horses and other animals for over one-hundred years, her property was grandfathered in under the old rules." That had been a burr in his side since he'd started trying to sell his grandmother's home.

Mrs. Chester wasn't the first potential buyer to object to living next to The Red Star Ranch. He had the feeling she wouldn't be the last, either. She didn't seem all that thrilled with his Gram's house in general, but he tried to salvage things anyway. "She's very respectful of the neighbors, keeps the noise and smell down, and isn't the type to have crazy parties or anything." He needed to get the woman's focus off the ranch and onto the house itself. "What do you think of the sun room? It's my grandmother's favorite room in the house. Warm and toasty in the winter, not too hot in the summer thanks to the tree that shades that part of the house."

"Yes, very nice." She barely glanced at the room as she headed for the front of the house. "The house layout is nice enough. I could deal with removing the wheelchair lifts, but I don't like animals. I'm afraid this won't work for us. Thank you for taking the time to show me around." She was on the porch in seconds, not pausing to say goodbye on the way to her car.

Jonah wanted to growl. This was the fourth buyer who had objected to the ranch next door. When he pointed out the lack of smell, two of them had reminded him that it was December in ski country, not July, and the smell would be far worse when it was hot outside. He couldn't dispute that, though he'd rarely noticed a hint of smell during his visits. Kaya Fiedler may have inherited the place rather than earning it, and she might have her quirks, but she took good care of the animals. He supposed she would have to if she wanted to keep her animal therapy license.

He'd seen up to six horses over there at a time before, but not recently. He wasn't sure if she had sold one, or if some were just inside when he looked over. He didn't spend that much time checking out the ranch.

Between his grandmother's health and all of the time he spent working to get his business off the ground, he had enough on his mind. If he didn't sell the house soon, he might have to rent the space over the gallery where he was living now, so he could pay the mortgage here. His grandmother couldn't afford both the mortgage and the assisted living center where he was trying to move her.

He watered the ficus before he double-checked the locks on the doors and windows and headed out. It was breaking his grandmother's heart to sell her home, but she couldn't live here alone anymore and he worked too many hours to be here as much as she would need. Ora Owen was a proud woman, and determined to be independent—which is why she broke her hip and was currently in a rehab center. If only she had moved to assisted living two years ago when he first urged her to do so.

He checked his watch—Mrs. Chester had been thirty minutes late. That was thirty minutes he couldn't afford to have missed from the gallery today. He'd have to put off that trip to fill his grandmother's Christmas list until later in the week instead.

"I can't believe you call this organized. Start over." Cecilia's strident voice rose loud enough for Kaya to hear her from the next department. Kaya felt a pang of empathy for Anika, who was a hard worker. If the place was a mess, chances were it was because of a customer, not because Anika had done anything wrong. Then again, Cecilia sometimes freaked out over the smallest disarray, even if the rest of the department was flawless. She was one miserable woman.

Kaya thought Cecilia could really use a cat to snuggle up with and take the edge off.

"Isn't that display finished yet?" Cecilia snapped, now standing behind Kaya.

Kaya turned to look over her shoulder at the older woman, her dark gray hair seemed to crackle with her bad temper. "I had to stop to assist a few customers." She kept her tone apologetic, though she wanted to growl and snap back. She had worked holidays at Kenworth a few times over the years, but never under Cecilia Grange. The woman was impossible. If Kaya didn't need the paycheck so badly, she would kick the woman in the shins and walk out. And to think she had once considered herself lucky to get the job.

Then again, a temporary, part-time position had been pretty lucky. The horses would run out of feed if she didn't get more holiday hours in. She had always liked this job in the past. It was a change of pace from her struggling equine therapy business, and since she had lost a few clients thanks to the rising prices of gasoline and the winter weather, she had to work on the side so the horses would have food. Otherwise she would have to sell one of them. Or both goats. And she desperately didn't want to do that. She had thought that nearly three years into her animal therapy business she would be making enough money to get her through the year, but it had been a tough fall.

Cecilia's beady eyes glared over the tops of her glasses. "You're all just full of excuses. Get back to work, and don't get so distracted. If you're going to take breaks while you're on duty, I'm going to start counting them as your scheduled ones." She turned and marched off.

Kaya bit her tongue and turned back to the display. She didn't know why the board of directors didn't kick the woman to the curb; she was so unprofessional. Not only could the neighboring employees hear, but several customers as well. And Kaya *hadn't* been taking breaks on the job, she'd been working hard. Which is more than Kaya could say for Cecilia, who seemed to do nothing but walk around, take two-hour lunches, and complain.

Biting back her anger, Kaya acknowledged that the woman must do something worthwhile or why would they keep her on staff? It was just not clear what she actually accomplished besides making all of the employees miserable.

This job only ran through New Year's Day, Kaya reminded

herself. She could put up with anyone for another month. Especially since the alternative was losing one of her horses.

It was only a few weeks and then the holidays would be over and the job would be gone, so she would suck it up and deal with it, for now. But she was going to tell Keira what she thought of the old bat before she left. Keira may not be over Cecilia, technically, but it was her family's store, so she had to have some kind of pull with the board.

Someone needed to get rid of Cecilia before she chased off all of the good employees.

Chapter Two

KAYA SMILED AS THREE OF HER favorite people walked up to the barn in her backyard late that afternoon. Her life may not have been ideal, but the Shoemakers came to her place, rain or shine, through all but the worst blizzards. "Hello, how are you all doing today?"

"Great, I can't wait to see how my girls are doing." Shyanne said from her wheelchair. She was nearly fourteen now and had fallen in love with Kaya's dairy goats—Jet Star and Morning Star. Their mother was the show-winning Yellow Star, and she hadn't been able to keep from buying goats whose names worked with her ranch. Kaya had been teaching Shyanne to milk the goats, since milking time was during their session, and she'd shown an interest.

Sasha, Kaya's Great Pyrenees, a livestock-guardian dog, gamboled over, greeting the three visitors happily.

Shyanne's younger brother, Chad had physical and social disabilities, though he wasn't wheelchair bound. He had fallen hook, line, and sinker for the horses the very first time their mother had brought them to check the place out.

Their monthly fee didn't hurt either. Their mom, Evelyn, had even recommended Kaya's services to several of the other clients who now came regularly to the ranch, which had been a huge blessing in the beginning when Kaya had been living on credit cards and income from her graveyard shift stocking shelves at the local Target.

Even without that, they would have been some of her favorite people—they were each a ray of sunshine in their own way. She ushered them into the barn.

Shyanne didn't even have to call to the goats. When they heard her voice, they came running through the door into the protected area in the barn, bleating a welcome. She rolled her wheelchair over and rubbed their heads through the fencing. "Hey, there, girls. How are you today? I brought you treats." Her hands went into her pockets and came out with a few twisty pretzels—one of their favorite snacks.

"I'll get her settled," Evelyn said.

"Thanks." Kaya walked over to Chad, who was looking down and brushing the toe of his shoe over the cement floor. "Are you ready to see the horses? Pepper is anxious to see you."

He nodded, stammering. "I saw her when we were outside. She was running around the paddock. She likes to run."

"Yes, she does. Someday maybe you'll be ready to run with her. Today, though, let's just get you on her back and riding. Can you help me saddle her up?" When he first started coming, she had Pepper, a sweet, gentle, red chestnut, all decked out with saddle and blanket. After a few weeks, she had him help take the saddle off of Pepper and brush her down at the end. The previous month they had graduated to him helping saddle her and remove the saddle afterward. He was nearly twelve and taking the responsibility of caring for the horse was part of Chad's treatment. Kaya sent monthly reports to his therapist so he would know how things were going on her end.

Chad walked over to the wall, collecting the heavy saddle with his wiry arms. She watched as he took it over to the gate into the paddock and laid it across the top, then returned for the bridle, blanket and other items.

Pepper met them at the fence and Chad climbed over, petting the horse, checking her for any injuries before he started to saddle her up. Kaya watched him go through the process making sure that he did it right, and then checked all of the buckles and connections herself when he finished.

She gave him a high five. "That was terrific. You did a great job. I didn't have to tighten anything. You're set. Mount up."

Chad grinned. It was the first time he had done it all correctly by himself and she could see the joy the accomplishment gave him. He led Pepper closer to the fence and used it to mount her, then rode off around the paddock.

"He's showing so much progress," Evelyn said as she joined Kaya at the fence.

Kaya had to agree; it gave her so much satisfaction. "Are you seeing an improvement in other areas as well?"

"We are. His teacher commented on it recently. It's helping him to deal with a lot of other areas in his life. He just needed the confidence."

Confidence wasn't the only area where he needed help. "How are things with the other kids at school? Is it getting any better?"

Evelyn let out a low breath of frustration. "No. I think we need to move so he can have a fresh start. I just don't think we can get the help we need in that district. They're doing fine with Shyanne—her disabilities are all physical and she copes well, plus she's so social and friendly with everyone. But the teachers and programs just aren't working for Chad. My parents keep trying to convince us to move out near them. Their schools are a little better, but it just feels wrong. I can't imagine tearing them away from here."

"Arizona is so far away." Kaya's heart sank at the suggestion. She would miss getting to see them so often.

"I know. But we can't keep living at the apartment where we're at now. Shyanne is getting so big. I'm afraid I'm going to hurt my back lifting her in and out of the wheelchair. She's working out so she will be able to do most of it herself, but she's not there yet, and may not be for quite a while. I knew we wouldn't stay there forever, I just didn't count on it being an issue so quickly. I can't seem to find a flexible job—even part time—so I can qualify to buy a house that would be easier for her. My ex is settling down with a new wife and kids and can't, or won't, help out more than he already is."

"I'd hate to have you go." Kaya paused to call out a correction to Chad. Though she was talking to his mom, she kept her eyes on him at all times. "As soon as it warms up here, I have several families who've committed to group lessons. I think Chad is comfortable enough that he's ready to work with other kids. I think it could be good for him socially, and the group will be small, no more than four at a time." She'd miss the pay from his private lesson if he switched to group, but it was the next step, and he was nearly ready for it. Maybe she should try a group social with several of her private clients and see how they meshed. That might help with the transition. She'd have to think about that in January.

"Mom, we need a goat. I like their milk better." Shyanne called from the pen. She brushed Morning Star, paying special attention to her flank, which, oddly enough, was the goat's favorite place to be caressed.

"That's another thing our apartment can't handle." Evelyn said it like a joke, but there was pain in her eyes. They needed a house with a yard and animals for the kids to keep advancing.

"You ever thought about moving closer to here instead?" Kaya asked. "I could use a full-time goat groomer, and my neighbor is selling." Not that she wanted Ora to move to that assisted living center, but it looked inevitable.

Evelyn shot her a tired look. She was maybe in her late thirties, and with her sandy-colored hair, smooth skin, and blue eyes, seemed somehow even younger than that, though she seemed worn out at the moment. "More times than you can imagine. I've been online looking at places, but nothing really stands out. The kids would love it. I've even heard good things about the school system, but a mortgage is going to take more income than we're getting from Glen plus Shyanne's social security and it can be hard to find a decent job when I never finished my degree." She sighed. "I'll figure it out." She lifted her voice again to call encouragement to her son.

Kaya wondered what Evelyn studied in school, but Chad waved

that he was ready for the next step. Maybe they could talk more later. "Looks like he's warmed up and ready to go."

"I'll help Shyanne set up to milk," Evelyn said, heading away.

Kaya vaulted over the railing and into the paddock to join him. "Hey, you ready to try a canter?"

"I don't know," Chad said.

"Let's give it a test and see how you like it. It's jiggly, though."

Chad looked a little dubious, but took to the faster speed like a pro.

Kaya ached when she thought of not seeing this kid again, but she had him for now. She'd have to do what she could while the opportunity was still there.

Chapter Three

JONAH SNATCHED UP THE TELEPHONE receiver, wishing it would stop ringing long enough for him to finish paying his bills. He wanted to let it go to voicemail, but the driver delivering his picture-framing supplies was supposed to call when he reached town.

He hadn't made it into Kenworth's yet to pick up the items his grandma had requested. He checked his watch again to make sure he would have time for it before the truck was supposed to arrive. He'd have to do it soon.

"Echo Ridge Arts, how can I help you?"

"Jonah, this is Mike. You left a message for me?" Mike was an old friend, a neighbor of Jonah's grandma, Ora, and had shown the house a few times when Jonah was tied up with other things.

Jonah's head lifted, as all thought of his spreadsheet left his head. "Yes, it's been a few days and I hadn't heard what your friends thought of the house." He had to sell Gram's house, and soon, or she was going to lose everything.

"They loved the house, it's just the right size, the layout is good, and the location couldn't be better, except for one thing."

Jonah had a sneaking suspicion he knew what that one thing was. "The horses?"

"Yes, they're concerned about noise and smells during the summer, even though I told them it wasn't an issue. They settled on a different house instead. Sorry."

That was exactly what he didn't need to hear—the neighbor's horses were variables he had no control over. "Thanks anyway."

"No problem. How is the gallery coming? Are you going to be ready?"

"It's coming along. We're nearly set for the opening show—I've gotten in some beautiful sculptures from a college friend, and I've been gathering some fantastic pieces from locals, plus I have a few other artists who are shipping me some amazing drawings and paintings. If I only had an extra six hours per day, I wouldn't worry about getting through it all." It used to be that he burned off his frustration and energy with his paints, but it had been a long time since that had satisfied him.

"Well, don't work too hard. Sarah and I will be there opening night, and it would be good if you weren't stuck in the hospital from a nervous breakdown."

"No kidding. Catch you later." They said goodbye and Jonah returned his gaze to the computer again, though he barely saw it. How many showings would he have to do before the house finally sold? Could he sell it with the animals next door?

He cleared that thought from his mind and focused on what he could control. At least a little. Just a few more bills to pay and he'd be done—and almost entirely out of money. He sure hoped the feelers he'd put out with art collectors he'd met over the years would pay off, because if he didn't sell a few pieces as soon as the gallery opened, his grandma wouldn't be the only one in dire financial straits.

Still, it could be worse. He was here, after all, in his own building, with a dream about to come true.

He finished paying the bills that were due before his gallery opening and turned off the computer. He would take an early lunch, do the shopping, go see Grams, and hopefully come back ready to get back to work with time to spare before the truck arrived.

His to-do list seemed to do nothing but grow every day. He stretched his back and groaned when several vertebrae popped back into place. He'd done a fair amount of the renovations himself, though he'd had an employee helping with some of the work. Sam had taken the day off for a family ski trip, so Jonah was solo today. Just as well, since the paperwork seemed never ending.

The roads had been cleared after the previous day's snowstorm, which thankfully had been only a few inches, despite the elevation in the ski resort town. Traffic was heavy—it was only three weeks until Christmas after all, and lunch time as well. He found a spot near the back of the Kenworth's parking lot and trudged into the building, freezing and wondering what he was going to do if he didn't find a buyer for his grandma's home. Her medical bills were piling up and he wasn't sure he would be able to handle the co-pay for the rehabilitation center where she was recovering from a broken hip.

If only the neighbor would keep her stinky horses somewhere else. As he entered the store, he glanced at the latest clothing styles in the men's department, hooked a left at the makeup counter and was passing the perfume when he stopped short. There was the source of all his trouble, touching all of the perfume bottles, like she couldn't decide which to buy. Her inheritance probably financed her little hobby farm so she could play around all day instead of doing real work. Animal therapy—like that was a real thing. Meanwhile his grandmother could lose everything, and it was Kaya's fault.

He stopped behind her. "Just can't decide which scent to buy next? I bet you need a lot to cover up the stink of those horses." The words popped out of Jonah's mouth before he could think better of it. He knew he should keep his mouth shut and walk on by, but he couldn't help venting on someone.

The woman turned, her dark eyes and smooth olive skin looking like she just came from shooting a commercial for natural beauty, her lustrous brown hair fell in waves halfway down her back. He could see the Spanish heritage from her Argentinian mother. She wore a professional navy skirt and white blouse with a clunky, golden necklace. Far cry from the dun-colored coveralls he'd seen her in last time he'd glimpsed her over the fence.

She brushed the hair back from her face and her brow wrinkled in surprise. "What do you mean?"

Thankfully his better judgment kicked in so he shut his mouth for a long moment, glaring at her. Ora would not appreciate him harassing Kaya, even if she deserved it. "Never mind." He moved past, headed for the toy area to pick out the gift his grandma had specified for his cousin's son.

Her hand snaked out and grabbed his sleeve. "No, not *never mind*. What was that about?"

He whirled and towered over her. "My grandma can't sell her house, thanks to you and those stinky animals. But you're only thinking about yourself, aren't you? Who cares about anyone else in the neighborhood?" He whirled away and stalked around the corner.

She let him go.

He may have been mad, but he didn't miss the look of shock that had crossed her face, and as he reined in his anger, he justified his actions, even though he should have held his tongue. Shouldn't someone tell her that her animals were a problem, that they were causing trouble? Was it fair to her to think everything was fine when it wasn't?

Jonah continued this mental tirade as he found the dump truck his grandma had wanted him to pick up, and then grabbed a board game for his own gift. By now he was starting to feel calmer and when his eye caught sight of the Hope Tree, sitting across the aisle from the toys, he couldn't help but go over to it.

Little cream-colored snowflake cards hung from the white flocked tree, far more than he would have thought a small town like this would have. This many people wouldn't have a decent Christmas without help? He looked at the cards.

Boy's pants, size 8.
Doll for six-year-old girl.
Toy horse for four-year-old boy.

He moved on from that one, settling on one that requested a chess set and another asking for art supplies for a budding artist. He didn't have much, but he could help with these, couldn't he? He'd been through the store and knew the art supply items couldn't be found here, but he could order some online. He tucked both cards into his pocket, then headed back to the toy aisle for the chess set before he took the toys he'd picked out to the cash register to check out.

When he glanced back over his shoulder at the perfume department across the store, he didn't see Kaya.

Apparently he'd chased her off. He wasn't sure how he felt about that.

Kaya stared after Jonah, confused about where his attack had come from. They had only met once since he'd moved back to Echo Ridge in the fall, though she'd seen him checking on his grandmother and then Ora's home after she ended up in rehab. She shouldn't care what Jonah Owens thought, but she pushed back the edge of hurt his words had caused and returned to organizing the fragrance display. Cecilia would get angry if she thought Kaya was slacking on the job, and it wasn't like she had to do anything wrong to bring the woman's anger down on her head. Considering how her future income looked at the moment, she couldn't afford to take any risks.

She felt bad that her therapy animals were making it hard for Ora's house to sell. She hadn't realized that was an issue, but she didn't think she was being the least bit selfish. The kids needed those animals—and so did she, if she had to admit it. Working with them brought her peace and satisfaction, not to mention her work with the disabled and how much spending time with the animals helped them. She was down to only four horses at the moment, though she'd been talking with someone about boarding their horse for the rest of the winter, which would definitely help her financially.

She let out a mental huff as she moved to the next display, straight-ening it since someone had mixed things up. Jonah's grandma, Ora, had praised him constantly, but obviously she didn't really know him that well. Being a great painter—and she had seen his work, so she knew he was—didn't excuse his behavior.

He could be angry and upset if he wanted to. It had nothing to do with her. The jerk.

A customer came forward, asking for advice for buying some perfume for his wife. She smiled brightly and helped him look at several fragrances, pleased as he took his favorite to the cash register to purchase a few minutes later.

As she turned back to the perfume counter, she caught another glimpse of Jonah, he was easily over six feet tall so he towered over the displays. It didn't hurt that his bright red scarf was hard to miss, as were his bright blue eyes, angular face, and pensive expression. Her gaze lingered on his features for a moment as he approached the Hope Tree Anika had been decorating all morning. It was covered in cream-colored cards edged like a snowflake with information on them for people who needed a helping-hand for Christmas. He read several, then took two off and stuck them in his pocket. He shifted the toys in his other hand, and delved back into the toy aisle.

Huh. She felt the edge of her anger soften ever so slightly. She supposed Jonah wasn't a total jerk, not if he was willing to help the less fortunate when things were obviously not going as well as he'd like.

Not that it made her like him anymore after the way he'd spoken to her. Not a bit.

16

It was dinner time when Kaya arrived home. Thursday was the only day she could work through the afternoon, and Cecilia had taken advantage of it since she'd started Thanksgiving week.

Kaya's grandmother had given her the land and house, free and clear, when she died—not everyone in the family had been happy about that, but there had been substantial gifts to go around, and no one else needed or wanted the old property like Kaya did.

Since the animals needed feeding, she put on her mud boots and headed for the barn. She was a tad later than usual to milk the goats, and everyone else would need to be tucked in for the night—it was supposed to be very cold as the storm front rolled in for the weekend. Sasha padded over to greet her as soon as she stepped out the back door. Her happy bark said that everything was normal and all of her charges were safe.

Kaya peeked in on the chickens, smiling to see them all snuggled together on their perch, gave Morning Star and Jet Star, the goats, each a quick head rub in greeting and moved on to check the horses before milking.

"Hey there, sweeties, how are you all doing?" They each got a rub or pat as she spoke to them, whispering endearments and making sure they were all doing well.

She still had a decent-sized paddock system for summer, which she had split into four sections, rotating the horses and goats through the areas, along with a couple of pigs some years, so the grass had a little time to grow back between. Trees provided shade and forage for the goats and a variety of grasses had been planted over the years to provide a better diet for everyone. This helped cut way back on her feed bill, though it was nowhere near cutting out entirely. It didn't help at all in the winter when it was feet deep in snow—thus the need for the part-time job for Christmas. If only she could pick up a few more clients, then she wouldn't have to worry about making the feed bill.

After checking in on everyone, Kaya prepared the milking

station. She broke off some sprouted barley from the day's fodder rations and set it in the feed tray, then grabbed the clean bucket she used for milking. She let Jet Star into the milking area and blocked her in. Jet Star hurried onto the milking station, anxious to get to her daily sprouts, and to be relieved of the milk in her udder. Kaya blocked her neck in so she could get to work. After properly sterilizing the udder, she sat on her stool to milk.

Hand milking the two goats didn't take long, and she found that most days, it was a nice chance to wind down from the day and settle in. The sound of milk hitting the metal pail was nearly hypnotic, and she would sometimes talk to the goats. Both girls were pregnant and before long she would have to start drying them out in preparation for the births in a couple of months, but for now they provided oodles of milk for her, a neighboring family who couldn't handle cow milk, and the chickens, who loved the leftovers.

After finishing with Morning Star and Jet Star, and setting the milk in the fridge to cool, she fed and watered everyone else. She did one final check and said goodnight to her babies. Working all day with the animals was tiring, but dealing with customers during the Christmas rush was exhausting as well—just in its own way. She couldn't wait until the new year when she could stay home all of the time again.

As she prepared for bed, Kaya's mind wandered back to Jonah's comment about her making it harder to find a buyer for Ora's house. She would have to check with Ora when she saw her the next day. Who knew, there might be something she could do to ease that problem—not get rid of the horses, of course, but *something*.

Ora and Kaya's grandmother had been good friends for more than a decade before Grandma died and Kaya had moved in. Ora had stepped right into the grandmotherly role and made Kaya's transition so much easier when she moved to town. There was little Kaya wouldn't do to make things easier for the sweet old woman.

Even if it meant dealing with an unreasonable man like Jonah.

Chapter Four

THE SKETCH OF THE LOCAL MOUNTAINS Jonah saw as he flipped through his sketch pad made him pause. He could remember the scene vividly, though it had been two years since he'd sketched the picture. He had envisioned a painting of it at the time, but then Janet had her accident and he hadn't gotten back to it. Feeling hopeful, he pulled up the watercolor paper and began to draw in the outlines, but nothing came together the way he wanted it to. The lines were right but they lacked any kind of emotion, or maybe that was him.

He was tired, probably too tired to do anything worthwhile, but he had to try. People talked about writer's block, but he'd had artist's block ever since Janet died. He *missed* his art, ached when he saw the beautiful things other people were creating. He missed them almost as much as he missed her. He couldn't get her back, and he couldn't live without art in his life. That's why he'd started the gallery.

He looked out the window and saw the snow piling up outside. He wasn't going anywhere in that weather, and his mind was too fuzzy to spend any more time pushing papers in the gallery. He'd put the final coat of shellac on the hardwood floor earlier that day, which meant he could start setting up the displays on Monday—he could hardly wait to see it all come together.

He stared at the watercolor paper in front of him, then gave up and put it away. Not painting was eating him up inside. He knew some people who found it easier to create when their life was in turmoil—their work took on a different edge as they spilled their fears, grief, or anger onto the paper or canvas. He needed hope to create anything he'd be willing to sell, and it hadn't been in big supply. Still, he gave it another shot.

After drawing, erasing, and redrawing didn't give him the results he had hoped for, he put his supplies away. It was late and he had a full day ahead of him.

He stretched, straightening his back, and rose, moving toward the window. He turned off the room light and stared out into the darkness. Snow had settled all around them and was still falling, coating everything in white. It was getting deep, the city snow plows had been running nearly non-stop since the previous day and it didn't look like the drivers would get respite in the next few hours.

Everything was beautiful and clean, at least for the moment. It wouldn't last long, though. With the rising of the sun, people would be rushing to their jobs. There would be slush and dirt and noise, messing it all up again.

And, apparently, he still wouldn't be able to create.

Losing his ability to paint felt like there was a big hole in his chest, growing bigger as time eroded it more every day. It was why he was opening the gallery instead of painting full time—maybe if he could be surrounded by art, use different creative skills to display it, he would slowly be able to fill that hole inside him. He just wished he'd decided to open the gallery at least six months earlier. That way he'd be open for business already and not in such a precarious financial position.

Jonah changed his clothes and got into bed, but all he could think about was what still needed to be done, so after ten minutes he rose again and headed to his makeshift office in the next room. Maybe if he got through some more of the paperwork piled up on his desk, he would be able to sleep that night.

Jonah heard laughter as he approached his grandmother's door in the rehabilitation center, then an odd sound like a soft whine. Another female voice chimed in and he rounded the corner.

At first he stepped into the room, not realizing what he was seeing. Then he stopped in shock, seeing his grandmother, lying in bed, holding a chicken. It was orange and fluffy and sat calmly in her arms, making a soft clucking sound while Kaya sat beside the bed, talking and smiling. She looked up, laughter still in her voice as she finished her sentence. Her smile disappeared when she saw him.

"What in blazes is going on here?" Jonah looked from the chicken to his grandmother to Kaya and back. "Chickens do not belong in a nursing home."

Kaya glared at him. "It's a rehab center, not a nursing home. And Bella is a certified therapy chicken."

"A *therapy* chicken?" He couldn't believe his ears. "That dirty, nasty, smelly thing is *therapy?*"

Kaya stood up to him, though she was at least six inches shorter than him. Her dark brows were pulled down in anger. "Bella is *not* dirty, nasty or smelly. She was thoroughly bathed just a couple of hours ago. She loves to be held and petted, and your grandmother—along with a number of other people who live here—loves her."

"A therapy chicken cannot be legit. Who gave you permission to bring that thing in here?" Recently bathed or not, the woman obviously had no sense. "What if it poops all over the blanket?" As soon as the words were out of his mouth, he realized they had rigged up a diaper of sorts for the bird, but still. It was gross.

"What kind of idiot do you think I am? I wouldn't let your grandma get pooped on." Kaya's voice went steely as she stared him down. "The head of the rehab center approved the chicken, because Bella is credentialed, just like a service dog, saying that she's been trained and behaves appropriately."

That made no sense. How could they train a chicken? "You've got to be kidding me."

"Jonah, sit down and calm yourself." Ora shot him an imperious glare and he sat as he was bidden. He wouldn't dare do differently, even if he was still upset.

"I love to see Bella. Kaya used to bring her to see me all the time when I was still at home."

"You like that bird?" he asked, confused.

"Of course. She's a sweetheart, aren't you Bella? Yes." She spoke to the bird in soft tones, stroking it with the tip of one withered finger. "We're good friends. Mr. Taylor likes you too, doesn't he? He pretends to be an old battle-ax, but he's a softie when it comes to you. Because you're a sweetheart."

Jonah stared. How could anyone consider a chicken *sweet?*

"Do you know what Kaya does for a living?" Ora asked after a moment.

"Of course. You've talked about her often enough." He turned to look at Kaya more closely. Today's outfit was less fancy, she wore less jewelry and seemed far more relaxed than she had while shopping a few days earlier.

"Then you know she's good at her job and wouldn't bring a smelly animal to me." Ora, apparently satisfied that they had come to an understanding, changed the subject, bragging to Kaya about Jonah's paintings and his gallery. Kaya appeared reasonably impressed, though it couldn't have been the first time she'd heard this about him. He'd certainly heard plenty about her over the past year or so. If she wasn't exactly impressed, then at least she didn't seem to think he was an idiot wasting his time, unlike some people he'd met. His work might not be philanthropic, but at least art was something he was passionate about.

When Kaya said she needed to move down the hall so Bella could visit the man Ora had mentioned, he was glad. He didn't have much time to spare and he'd rather have Grams to himself.

He glanced over his shoulder as Kaya disappeared down the hall, then back at his grandmother. She wore a happy smile. It was clear she held a lot of affection for the younger woman, but Jonah didn't care about her therapy work—he just cared that his grandma could lose everything after all these years. Thanks to her stinky animals.

Chapter Five

"I'M HEARING COMPLAINTS ABOUT YOU," Cecilia said to Kaya as soon as the customer Kaya had been helping turned to walk away. She didn't even let the man take three steps. He glanced back over his shoulder at them, speculation entering his expression, but then he moved on.

Kaya gritted her teeth. She wasn't sure how much more of this she could take. "Really?"

"Apparently you couldn't help someone find the perfume he wanted. He said he spent nearly half an hour with you and you were useless."

Kaya instantly knew who Cecilia was talking about. He had been in there just before the previous customer and demanded a huge chunk of time, then bought nothing. The florals were too floral, the musks were too musky. He didn't like the light body sprays because you had to get too close to the person to smell them and the few fruity scents they had in stock were too sweet. Kaya was convinced he had time to kill and hadn't intended to buy anything to begin with. "I showed him every one of our scents. Apparently we don't have anything in stock that pleases him. I did try my best to help him find something he liked."

"Hmmm, well, I don't want to hear any more complaints like that one." She looked past Kaya at the stack of boxes behind her. "And why isn't that inventory on the shelves yet? It looks like you haven't even started."

Seriously? How many hands did she think Kaya had, anyway? "I've been busy with customers." Hadn't Cecilia just gotten on her case about how long she spent with one of them?

Cecilia frowned, her brows furrowing in distaste. "You won't be working mornings anymore. It's not effective. I'll have you starting in the afternoons tomorrow."

Kaya panicked. "I can't do that. I have clients most afternoons. That's why I'm working mornings."

A gleam entered Cecilia's eye. "If you can't work when I need you, then you'll need to find a different job."

"When I was hired through the temp agency, I specifically mentioned that I have appointments in the afternoon. I was told that wouldn't be a problem, that you could work around it."

Cecilia sniffed. "Apparently they didn't check with me first. Be here tomorrow afternoon or don't bother to come back. The new schedule is posted in the break room." She looked at Kaya, smug, and walked off.

Kaya signaled to Lola, one of the other temps, to come cover the perfume area, hoping to get away and check the schedule. If it was just one afternoon, or a couple of set afternoons per week, maybe she could reschedule the clients. She told Kenworth's she was free on Thursday afternoons, after all. She sucked in deep breaths, staving off her panic as best she could, but must have overdone it because by the time she skirted the Hope Tree, crossed the toy aisle, and walked back to the employee area, she was starting to feel light-headed.

And then she saw the schedule. Every weekday afternoon *except* Thursdays until New Years Day. Every. Single. One.

Kaya wanted to throw something. Cecilia had been gunning to get rid of her from the beginning. This was done deliberately to get Kaya to quit, since Cecilia had no grounds to fire her. A few curse words escaped and she had to step out the back door into the cold to keep from crying. Why did that old witch have to be so nasty?

The air was frigid and the wind whipped around her, blowing

25

across her neck. She let out a short, quieter scream of rage than she would have liked, then filled her lung with fresh air before going back inside to deal with life. She would have to quit, but at least she could finish out her shift.

She called the temp agency and told them what happened and that she would finish her shift, but that was it. She also stopped into HR to let them know what happened. Then she called up from HR's phone and left a message for Cecilia on her voicemail that she would have to find someone else to fill the slots.

Kaya returned to her post, smiling and joking with customers as best she could, but all of the holiday spirit had melted out of her.

She would survive. Maybe she could pick up a shift or two per week at one of the boutiques in town for the rest of the ski season. Something was bound to come up. She hoped.

Merry Christmas indeed.

Jonah stared at the invoice and wondered where he was going to come up with the money. Was there any prayer that he would make enough in the opening two weeks of the gallery to actually pay the incoming bills? Never mind the artists' commission on top of the expenses. His friends were putting a lot of trust in him and he didn't want to let them, or himself, down. He didn't know how to do anything but draw and paint—or at least that's what he'd believed. When he lost that, he'd realized he had learned a few things at his college job, and there was this option.

If he hadn't made so many contacts and so many friends, the gallery wouldn't have been an option. Only now he had to make good on his promises, and with a little over a week until the gallery opened, he wasn't sure that was possible. If sheer desire could make it happen, he would have no need to worry, but that wasn't enough, and the prep on the building still wasn't done. He just hoped the advertising and word of mouth he'd been working on would bring people in—no matter what condition the building was in on opening day.

He filed the invoice to deal with after he'd made a deposit or two then walked back out to the showroom. The work to restore the space had finished only a week earlier, and he'd been busy framing pictures and uncrating items since. It was going slower than he had expected. Then again, maybe that had something to do with Sam—his nineteen-year-old employee, who apparently seemed to think the start time for work was flexible.

Jonah sighed and checked his watch again. He only trusted the kid to work for a couple more days, and then he'd have to let him go. Sam wasn't a terrible employee, but he wasn't exactly stellar, either, and he wasn't someone Jonah trusted to handle some of the more valuable pieces—especially after some of the less graceful moves the kid had made: knocking over displays, dropping one canvas, and breaking one side support, making Jonah re-stretch it.

Jonah got back to work on a frame for one of his own paintings, one he'd done a couple of years earlier. It had been far too long since he'd put paint to canvas. Or maybe it had just been too long since he'd been able to do anything that wasn't plain mediocre. He ached for the way painting used to make him feel.

He looked at the painting of a mother and child playing in the park and remembered the way he'd planned the longer sweeping strokes, the care he'd used to select the perfect shades of color and the way instinct, coupled with years of practice had guided his hand. This piece had gotten attention at the previous gallery where it had been placed, but it was one of three pieces that hadn't sold during the consignment period, and when Jonah had been unable to produce anything else, the gallery owner had offered to let him take them back. Now he wasn't sure if it was more painful to see it as a reminder of what he'd lost, or more hopeful as a reminder that he might, someday, have it again.

He was almost loathe to sell the three final paintings, though he desper-ately needed the money.

Like painting, framing was both art and science, and took his concentrated effort. Thankfully, it didn't seem to need as much of the muse as painting had, though he could become just as engrossed. Another thirty minutes passed before Jonah thought about Sam again, then, irritated, he picked up his phone to call the kid.

Sam answered the phone, his words tripping over themselves. "Oh, Jonah, I'm so sorry. I should have called, I just wasn't thinking."

"You weren't thinking that you were nearly an hour late for work?" Jonah knew he wasn't succeeding very well at keeping the irritation from his voice.

"I was in an accident on the way there." His voice held a slightly shaky quality. "I didn't think to call you. I'm so sorry. It's been crazy."

Jonah set down the stack of matting samples, focusing closer on the conversation. "What happened, are you okay?"

"I broke my leg. The x-rays just came back. The doc says it's going to be a couple of weeks before I'm up and around. Even then I'll probably have crutches. I still have to get my cast. I'm sorry I won't be able to help you out any more."

Jonah felt bad for his earlier irritation. "Oh, man, that's terrible. Do you have someone there for you?" Not that he could afford to lose even a little more work time if Sam was already out of the picture, but no one deserved to sit at the hospital by themselves.

"My sister is coming from Albany to pick me up. I'll visit her for a while. My car is totaled. Not sure how I'll get around. Idiot driver hit me at the intersection."

"Don't worry about work. I'm sorry this happened to you. Take care of yourself." Jonah wished him well and ended the call. He did feel bad for Sam, but dang it, he didn't know what he was going to do without the help. Sam was only hired on a temporary basis, but Jonah went from somewhat overwhelmed to super stressed in a heartbeat. "Eighteen-hour days, here I come."

He remembered his grandma was expecting a visit in a little while and decided to put it off today. She would understand if he had to change his visiting schedule to every-other day until the gallery was up and running. The thought made him feel bad, but he didn't have much choice at this point.

He picked up the phone to call her.

Chapter Six

ORA LAUGHED, TIPPING HER HEAD back and letting it loose from her gut.

Kaya watched, glad the old woman had enjoyed her story, and to see her doing so much better. Ora and her own grandmother had been close friends in the years that they had lived side-by-side and Kaya was grateful for the friendship she had developed with Ora since she had moved into her grandmother's house. This morning she had needed a pick-me-up, since the search for local job openings had not been fruitful. Though it had been less than a day since she finished work at Kenworth's, she was already anxious about being out of work. It seemed everyone had hired for the holidays, and the temp agency hadn't had anything on the books for the near future that would work.

She could get through January on what she had earned so far, but winter in ski country lasted a lot longer than that, and she would definitely run out of feed before the snow melted. She had needed the visit with Ora as much as the older woman had needed to be visited.

"It's so good to talk to you. Thanks for stopping by," Ora said. "My Jonah comes by every day, but he's been so busy with getting the gallery open that sometimes it's only for ten minutes before they kick him out for the night."

"Sounds like he doesn't have much time to relax." She could relate. If she didn't have a second job, there were more than enough projects at home that needed attention. Cheese making was at the top of her list for the day—the goats would stop producing milk soon in preparation for giving birth and if she wanted the fantastic goat cheddar she'd come to love so much, she needed to get on it while she had plenty of milk. And then there were fence repairs and other work outside.

"No, he definitely doesn't have a lot of spare time." She shook her head sadly. "My Jonah says he'll take a break when the gallery is running. But I'm sure he isn't considering the work it takes to keep a place like that running, especially if he's going to start painting again."

Kaya was surprised. She knew Jonah was an artist—Ora wasn't the least shy about bragging on him—but Kaya hadn't been aware that he'd taken a break from it. Maybe that was just because of getting the gallery launched. "It's easy to underestimate how much time paperwork and taxes can take up." Getting her animal therapy business off the ground had not been a picnic, and keeping up with taxes, certifications and the myriad other things that came with it wasn't much better.

The phone beside the bed rang and Ora answered it. "What? Oh, no! Is he all right? That's too bad. Of course. Yes, I understand. I'll see you tomorrow instead. Love you, honey." She glanced at Kaya and smiled. "Hold on, Jonah." She covered the mouthpiece on the phone. "Didn't you say you needed a part-time job through the end of the year?"

"Yes. There isn't much available right now, though. Especially that's flexible enough for me to work with my clients."

Ora beamed. "I have something for you." She uncovered the phone and spoke to Jonah. "I know just the person to help you out. I'll send them right over. No problem. Love you and I'll see you tomorrow." She said goodbye and hung up.

"Jonah called to say he's not going to make it tonight. He had a part-time helper and the kid was in a car accident, broke his leg." She shook her head. "He won't be able to work again until after the gallery has opened. Jonah really needs an extra hand and he doesn't have the luxury of being picky about your hours if you're willing to work. He needs someone he can count on to do what needs to be done without whining about it. I know you can be that person."

Kaya was touched that Ora had such a high opinion of her—and extremely grateful, even if it meant working with Jonah. She shrugged it off. If she could put up with Cecilia's attitude for the past couple weeks, she could handle Jonah. "Thanks. I guess I better go." Kaya was stunned that it could be that easy. She hoped Jonah really was desperate enough for help that he didn't balk when he saw that it was her.

The gallery was down Main Street a block or so from Kenworth's, and only a few blocks from the rehab center where Ora was staying. Kaya found a parking spot in the lot out back and came around to the front entrance. There was a back entrance, but she didn't know if he would hear her knocking, so decided to try the front door first. It was locked, of course, but when she knocked on the glass, Jonah stepped out from behind a wall and walked over. "We're closed for another week," he said when he opened the door enough to be heard.

She chose not to be irritated at his attitude. "I know, I'm here to help. You told Ora that you needed another set of hands. She sent mine." She lifted her hands, holding the palms up as evidence.

He seemed nonplussed. "Oh, she didn't say it was you." His eyes narrowed and he looked around her, suspiciously. "Do you have the chicken here?"

She held in a chuckle. "No, I don't take her to the rehab center every time I visit your grandma. Besides, I had other errands here in town this morning. I can only work until two-thirty today, but I can come in whenever you need me tomorrow morning and work about as late."

"Well, good." He stood for a moment longer, as if trying to decide whether to let her in or not, then stepped back. "I can definitely use the help. Let's see how things go today and tomorrow and take it from there." He quoted the amount he could pay her and she agreed. It was actually a little better than she had been getting at Kenworth's.

Kaya worked until half an hour before her therapy client would arrive at her place, then headed home to prepare. Most of her clients were in school, so most of her appointments were between three and six during the winter.

She had been surprised at how smoothly things went with Jonah. She had lifted and carried with him, helped him open crates, and listened to him muse about the correct lighting for each piece they had considered. Even though she only worked for a couple of hours, it was every bit as exhausting as a day repairing paddock fencing.

Jonah had started out a little gruff, like he thought she was going to balk at the things he had her do. As she worked hard without complaint, however, he seemed to appreciate her work ethic and started to soften. She just hoped it would continue the next day.

Chapter Seven

JONAH HAD BEEN SURPRISED AT how smoothly the unpacking and displays had come together with Kaya's help—much better than with Sam, who had dragged his feet every step of the way and had apparently never heard of the word initiative.

Kaya was completely different. He felt like an idiot, thinking she was some prima donna—of course she would be strong and hard-working, he'd never seen his grandma become friends with anyone who was spoiled or lazy. Kaya had worked hard for the three hours she was with him the previous day, then gone home to do some therapy sessions.

Now as he pulled into the driveway at her place, he noticed someone was there, probably one of her patients... clients... whatever she called them. He parked to the side so he didn't block them in and circumvented the house, heading to the barn behind it. In the snow and mud-laced practice ring connected to the barn, he found a kid of eleven or twelve riding Kaya's sorrel horse.

He walked over to the horse fence and leaned his forearms on it, watching Kaya interact with the child on the horse, calling out instructions and encouragement as the boy grinned, holding tightly to the saddle horn.

Jonah had a sudden flashback to being a teenager and looking over the fence from his grandmother's yard. A young girl—three or four years younger than himself—had been riding her horse around the ring, calling back to her grandmother "Look at me! I'm doing it!"

Her grandmother stood at the railing, on the outside, beaming as she watched the young girl handle the horse on her own.

He blinked, letting the memory fade as he focused on the people before him. He studied Kaya across the paddock. Had it been her all those years ago? He wasn't sure, but it could have been. She was about the right age, with the same dark hair. Kaya's face had lit up with the same bright joy at the boy's success that he'd seen on the younger girl so long ago. How had he forgotten the way that stolen peek had made him yearn? That was a kind of happiness he'd not seen often, and definitely not in his own life up to that point. His father had been firmly against art as a career—he probably felt vindicated about that now, though they rarely spoke.

He heard gravel crunching behind him and looked over his shoulder to see a woman who was a little older than himself. The boy had her eyes.

"She's great with him, isn't she?" the woman asked.

"Yeah."

"Are you a neighbor?"

"Not really. My grandma is. Kaya's working for me right now. Temporarily." He gestured to the ring. "Is he your son?"

"Yes. You wouldn't believe how much he's changed since she started working with him last spring. It's amazing. And my daughter, she's in with the goats, she just lights up when we come here. It's amazing."

Jonah looked back at the boy in the ring with new eyes. He saw the joy of success radiating from the boy's face, as well as Kaya's joy at working with him and he felt that icy wall that he'd built between himself and Kaya melt just a bit more.

The session ended and Jonah hung back as he watched Kaya talk things over with the mother and boy, as well as a girl a year or two older than the boy, who rolled out in her wheelchair. He hadn't expected that, but he supposed it explained why she was hanging out with the goats. On her lap, she carried a bulging canvas bag.

They took the horse back into the barn, and he followed close enough to see Kaya assisting the boy in removing the saddle and other equipment from the horse. The older girl fed each of the goats something from her hand, obviously in love with the smaller animals. He shifted back away from the door before anyone noticed him.

He hadn't seen Kaya look in his direction since he had come into her yard, but as soon as the family was headed for their van, Kaya turned and looked straight at him. "I didn't expect to see you here."

He walked around to her. "I like to check in on Gram's place every few days. It's been a few. I saw you had a client so I thought I'd see what it is you do."

"It probably doesn't look like much here, but working with the animals is making a difference for Chad and Shyanne."

"It doesn't look like nothing. I can tell you love it, and so do the kids. When did you decide you wanted to get into this kind of work?" For the first time, he actually wanted to understand her.

"I do love it. I first heard of equine therapy when I was still in high school, I was doing a paper for English and thought it would be a good topic. I was fascinated. The more I learned, the more I knew that's what I wanted to do. Grandma agreed, which made all of this much easier." She gestured expansively to include the property. "I was lucky she left me the house and grounds so I could pursue my dream. I don't know how I ever would have made enough money to do this otherwise, not for years." Kaya stood with her back to the railing and the horse came over to nibble on the shoulder of her coveralls. She smiled and lifted a hand to press against the side of its face, stroking as she looked up at the horse. "You're a sweetie, aren't you? She's so good with the kids. It's amazing how an animal can change a person's life. They changed my life, and they are making a difference for both of those kids."

Jonah was touched by how passionate Kaya was about her job and her animals. "That's how I feel about art. Using it to express yourself when you're happy, sad, depressed, or anything else." Not that depression worked for him, but he knew people who produced great art in that state of mind.

"Thus the gallery. What are you going to do when it becomes fabulously successful and you don't have time to paint?"

In his wildest dreams! "Hire help. I'm hoping to find someone part-time who is willing to stay and learn the business—or better yet, who already knows something of the business and is willing to really dig into it. I'd offer a longer-term position to you after seeing you work the past couple of days, but I know you want to get back here." He certainly couldn't fault her work ethic.

"So much. Being away from it to work for you is hard, there are a ton of things that need to be done here, but most of them will keep until next month." She shivered. "You probably need to go, and I ought to get the animals settled for the night. Shyanne already milked Morning Star, but Jet Star is probably ready and anxious for her turn, and there are other things to do."

"Need a hand? I could use a longer break before going back to the gallery." He was surprised at how much he wanted to see her setup inside.

"Great." Kaya led the way into the barn, showing him what to feed each of the animals and how much. She talked about when she got each of the horses and a little about their backgrounds, pausing to coo and stroke them each for a moment. It was clear how much she loved them, and that they loved her. The one the boy had been riding was fully divested of her gear and Kaya double-checked everything, then brushed the horse for a few minutes while Jonah fed the others. All the time, they kept up a conversation.

She seemed content with her life, even though it was just her and the animals. Jonah wondered if she got lonely—if that was why she visited the rehab center and nursing home with the chicken. Gram had mentioned Kaya a few times and he wondered how often she actually came to see the folks there, and how often she took the chicken with her. And how she thought of bringing a bird to visit instead of the usual dog.

He was surprised to see that she actually had a dozen chickens, two goats and a pen where she said she kept pigs in the spring.

"You have pigs?"

"Well, usually just two, through the warm months. I feed them the extra milk from the goats, as well as extra chicken eggs, and they roam the pastures. Then I sell one and a half in the fall to pay for feed for the goats and chickens all winter and buy new piglets in the spring."

"You eat the other half of the pig, though, right?"

"Yes. Best ham and bacon I ever tasted." She gave the horse a pat on the neck and came out, shutting the stall behind her. "There's a rancher in the area who does animal processing, not just pigs and cows but elk and deer in the fall. He's very good and has great prices. I can deliver the animals to him and he'll let the buyers pick up the finished meat from him. It makes it easy."

This fascinated Jonah more than he expected. Though he had painted a lot of outdoor scenes, he had always been a city boy. The move to Echo Ridge had been a real leap of faith for him. "I never noticed the smell of pigs last summer." He'd been up to visit to look for property several times before settling on the gallery space.

She shook her head, smiling, as she collected some equipment and took it over to a small platform near the goats. "Pigs don't have to stink, not if they have a large enough pen. And with the pasture, I only buy a little supplemental feed for them. The south grove has a lot of oak trees, so I run them through there for a couple months before butchering, I heard acorns make a huge difference in the taste of the meat. I have to say, I'm a convert."

"Sounds like they practically feed themselves."

"They nearly do." She grabbed a metal pail he had seen earlier and pulled off the close-fitting lid, then set it nearby. "In the summer they eat a lot of pasture. I rotate the animals through the field, and I've planted it in certain kinds of plants to make everyone happy, but

I always lose some clients in the winter because of the cold, and I go through a lot more feed."

"You didn't have enough to save to tide you over?" It didn't seem like her—she appeared very careful and deliberate.

She opened the gate to the goats and let one in, plopped a stack of some plant in the feeder, and locked the goat's head in place. "I generally set aside enough extra cash to float us over the winter, but I had unexpected expenses this fall. If I could afford the indoor arena I've been planning the past few years, it would make a difference for my clients, and I have a few clients who would love to board their horses here, if they could exercise them in a more sheltered area during the snow." By now she had cleaned the udder and was sitting on the stool to start milking.

Jonah wasn't sure if the arena would increase the problems with selling land adjacent to hers or not. Hopefully it wouldn't matter to him by the time she scrounged the cash to build. She did seem focused on keeping the smells under control. "Can you board horses in this neighborhood?" The sound of milk hitting the inside of the pail filled the air as they spoke and he noticed the way she leaned a little against the animal, as if she could transfer some of her affection for it that way. Maybe she could. He almost missed her response because of the thought.

"I'm zoned agricultural, even if no one around me is. I'm sure I can get approval for it, as long as I board only three or four. I just have to find the money to make it all work."

He tried to withhold judgment, though he wanted to ask why she would do that to everyone who lived near her. He settled on a less judgmental way to ask the question. "What do your neighbors think about your business? I mean having the animals here. I know some people are funny about that."

"Some think it's great, others don't love it quite so much." Kaya frowned a little. "I have ten acres and the arena would go pretty much in the middle, so it shouldn't cause much extra noise or smell for the neighbors, and because I rotate the animals on the field, especially because of the pigs, I only get stinky areas when it gets really wet—and I do my best to avoid it then. As it is, the arena won't be much bigger than the paddock here, but I know a few other people who would love to have one closer than Clover City."

Kaya rested her face against the goat's flank, her expression serene. Outside, through a window a few feet above her head, he could see the moon starting to rise, framed by snow in the windowsill. His heart did something strange in his chest as she hummed a few notes from a song he didn't recognize.

He watched and considered her plans as she finished milking the goat, filtered the milk and cleaned up. Maybe they wouldn't be so bad after all. Jonah walked her back toward the house. "Well, I appreciate your help at the gallery." They had finished taking care of the animals and were walking back to the front of the property. "I'll take off and let you finish up here."

She held his gaze for a long moment. "Thanks for the help with the evening chores."

"No problem. It was good to see some of what you do here. See you tomorrow." He waved goodbye and sauntered toward the door.

Before Jonah walked around the corner of the house, though, he glanced back at her, disappearing inside. He turned away, hurrying back to his car.

She was a constant surprise, with her goats and plans, and the bit of herself she displayed with every move. He didn't know what to think about her.

Chapter Eight

JONAH FINISHED SOME PAPERWORK after dinner, booked a viewing for the house on Saturday, and then sat on the sofa. The image of Kaya as a child lingered in his mind, over-laid with the child on the horse, and the teenager in the wheelchair. They had pulled emotions from him that he hadn't felt so strongly in a long time, so he grabbed a stick of charcoal and a sketch pad and started sketching out the paddock in Kaya's back yard. The horse was tall, majestic, the child on its back... not the twelve-year-old boy who had been riding that night. Instead, it ended up being Kaya as a young teen, or at least the way he remembered her. The face held only a little similarity to the way she looked now, but instinctively, his fingers glided over the paper.

The snow around the ring seemed to melt away in his mind as he remembered the autumn day, the tang in the air, the crispness of leaves under his feet. Who knew if the setting was even from the main memory, or if he had blended a second memory of the weather into the first? It may not have even been Kaya on that horse that day, but the preteen on the paper held enough similarities to her that it might well have been.

He turned to a new page, thought of the boy and started drawing him on the sorrel, his gangly arms and legs seemingly out of proportion with the rest of him as boys so often were at his age. Jonah didn't draw him straight on, but at an oblique angle, his excitement showing from the way he held his arms and legs, the implied movement of the horse. It felt a little like joy.

When he finished a rough draft, he flipped the sheet and started on one of the girl in the wheelchair and the happiness that had suffused her face as she held out a treat for the goat. It nuzzled her hand and she grinned brightly, joy on her face. She was detailed, and the goat was moderately detailed, but the rest of the space, the straw, the wooden beams and windows were little more than shapes in the picture, lines shooting off in different directions, adding dimension and mood without being fully formed.

It felt good to create, to feel the dust of charcoal, the sharp edges of the rectangular stick pressing into the pads of his fingers. His hands ached to hold a brush and spread paint across the paper, to see the form emerging from his mind and heart as he created something more than either part of him could ever do alone.

He hurried down to the back room of the gallery where most of his art supplies had been stored in perfect order, so he could find whatever he needed, almost without lifting his eyes from the watercolor paper while he worked.

He grabbed a pencil, soft and fine pointed, sketching the girl in the barn, outlining the important areas, shaping the face, the tumble of hair pouring below her knobby winter scarf. He grabbed the eraser, kneading it to remove the bits of graphite that had gone astray, then continued his outline.

Slowly the image came to the surface, and, finally satisfied, he switched to his watercolor paint. A little wash of tan, barely there, blocked around his white areas, showing him where the color would be divided from it. He worked from light to dark, reveling in the freedom to form shapes with color.

And then he had to stop. The paper had to dry properly, and he needed to stand and stretch. The stool where he sat was the wrong height for painting at and he'd been hunched over as he worked. He would have to find something else.

Jonah hadn't known if he would ever paint again. After losing Janet in that car accident, he had tried to paint, but it was as though his inspiration had disappeared and he hadn't produced anything decent since. The few works he'd tried were technically proficient, but definitely not inspired.

He still didn't know if this one would be more than proficient or not, but he was pleased with the charcoal study. He jotted a note on a bright yellow sticky note to get a better chair to sit in while he painted and tacked it to his computer screen. He glanced at the clock and blinked twice when he realized it was after two in the morning. It had been so long—*so long*—since he'd felt like that, he had lost all track of time.

No wonder his back hurt and his eyes felt gritty.

Wishing he could get back to work on a different image, but knowing he had a lot to do the next day, he locked up and went upstairs to his apartment for the night. With any luck, he'd be able to sleep and the next day he would feel like finishing that painting.

For the first time in over a year, he had some hope that he would be more than just a gallery owner again.

A funky nightmare where horses blamed Kaya for the weather woke her nearly an hour earlier than usual on Friday. Unable to get back to sleep, she got ready for the day, prepped the animals, and milked slightly ahead of schedule. Finding herself with time on her hands before work, she went out for a leisurely breakfast at a nearby restaurant—an unusual but occasional splurge to jump-start her day.

Even after taking her time over the eggs and hash browns, she showed up at the gallery fifteen minutes early. There was a light on in the back room, so she knew Jonah was already working. She was starting to wonder if he ever slept. She knocked on the back door and waited, rubbing her hands over her heavily covered arms, her breath turning to clouds in the air. He came to the door and frowned slightly. "You're early."

"I know. Sorry if I interrupted you on a call or something." She had no idea who he would be calling at this time of day, but you never knew. He was showered, freshly shaved, and wore a nice green sweater that brought out flecks in his blue eyes.

He held the door for her, then pulled it tightly shut behind them. It stuck sometimes and didn't like to close properly.

When she took off her coat, she glanced in the storage room and saw his easel set up, a blue pool of cloth lay over the edge of the table. But most interesting was the paper on the easel. It faced away from her, but she felt drawn to it. She took a couple of steps into the room. "Is that a painting smock?" She pointed to the fabric.

Jonah confiscated it, hanging it in a long, open cupboard, and she noticed he had a couple dabs of paint on his right thumb in blue and yellow. He shook his head. "I hadn't expected you for a few more minutes so I haven't started to clean up."

Kaya ignored him and walked around the easel to get a look at what he was doing. It wasn't finished, not nearly, but she could clearly see the outline of Shyanne feeding the goats. "Wow."

"It's not much yet." He set a nearby brush into the cup near the easel, and carried it with several other brushes over to the bathroom sink. "I sometimes take an hour or two in the morning to work on a painting before I get to work on the gallery. It helps calm my mind." His tone was very matter of fact, but his demeanor said he was nervous about something, maybe having her see his unfinished work?

She'd heard some artists could be like that. "I understand that. If I'm anxious about a new student or meeting a new family, sometimes I go out to the barn early and give one or two of the horses a solid brushing, just talk to them or the goats and let their serenity calm me."

He looked over and their gazes met, a feeling of pure understanding flowing between them. Something more, something strong, fluttered in her chest, undeniable. She glanced away, surprised that she could feel that way with him. He had been so standoffish to start with. Still was, sometimes. She wondered why.

Instead of dealing with it, she walked closer to the painting and studied it closer. There were no details on Shyanne's face, but Kaya could still sense the tilt of her chin. She couldn't wait to see the finished product. "This is really coming along. I've seen a couple of your other projects at Ora's. They're good. Very good. I'm surprised you don't paint full time."

He kept his back to her as he washed out the brushes, though she wasn't sure if the extra washing was strictly necessary or if he stayed at the sink to keep his hands busy. "I did paint full time for a while. I loved it, but it's hard to make a living that way. With this I get the best of both worlds." He never looked her in the eye and she wondered if he was hiding the truth, whatever it was.

She didn't feel like she knew him well enough to press the point, so she changed the subject and got to work.

Chapter Nine

JONAH WOKE UP EARLY the next morning, grabbed a coffee and leftover Danishes he'd bought next door at Fay's Café the previous evening and headed for his easel. It was Saturday, so Kaya had early clients. When he had spent an hour on the painting, he checked the clock and groaned. As much as he didn't want to leave his easel yet, he had an appointment to show Gram's house at ten, and was really hoping it would pan out this time. Though her spot had been approved at the assisted living facility, she was talking about moving home instead if the house didn't sell.

It would solve part of the financial issues, but the administrator of the assisted living facility said there were now three names behind hers on the waiting list, so if she didn't take the apartment, it could easily be six months or more before her name came up on the list again.

Jonah added a touch of blue to the girl's eyes in his painting, and cleaned up the brushes. He tried not to get his hopes up about the house selling. He'd shown it so many times already, and couldn't imagine this one turning out much better.

Fifteen minutes later he pulled up at the house and saw a familiar blue van in the driveway. The driver's door opened and the woman emerged, coming around to greet him. "Hi, I'm Evelyn. We met next door at Kaya's didn't we? I didn't realize you owned this place."

"Yes. I'm Jonah. I guess the horses and goats next door won't bother you, then?" He couldn't believe his luck on that end of things.

Plus the girl was in a wheelchair. If they liked the house layout, this could be perfect for them.

Evelyn laughed, looking younger than he'd remembered from their brief chat in the farmyard earlier that week. "Proximity to the horses is actually one of the perks of this place. And the wheelchair lifts you mentioned on the information sheet are another perk." She walked back to the van where her son had been helping her daughter onto the electronic lift that helped the wheelchair exit the van.

Shyanne—Kaya had mentioned her name when she saw the painting—looked up at him, happiness suffusing her face. "I really hope we can get your house. I love Kaya and her goats."

"I hope you love the house as much as my grandmother does. Why don't you come on in?" He walked around the wheelchair ramp he'd built for his grandfather nearly a decade earlier and unlocked the front door.

They *did* love the house. Evelyn thought the kitchen, modest by many standards, though more spacious than some, was wonderful. Everything was wide enough for Shyanne to navigate, and the master bedroom, which had the wheelchair lift by the bed, wasn't much bigger than the second bedroom, which Evelyn would take instead.

"You have no idea what a blessing it is to find this house—not just because of the proximity to Kaya," Evelyn said when they'd been through the whole place. "I need to check a few things to see if we can swing a mortgage, but I definitely want to make an offer if everything works out."

"I would love to sell it to you." Jonah said with a chuckle. "Not just because it would be great to get my gram settled into the assisted living center without worrying about a mortgage here. She loved this house. She and my grandpa built it and made wonderful memories. In so many ways, it's the home of her heart and I know she'll be happy knowing that you live here with your kids, loving it just as much as she did." He really hoped it worked out for them. It was a perfect fit from every angle he could think of.

"What do you do for a living? Do you live around here?" Evelyn asked as they exited through the front door a few minutes later.

Jonah locked the house up behind him. "I'm opening a gallery downtown this week." He glanced at Shyanne and made a decision. "I think you should come. I think you'll be pleasantly surprised." He wondered what she would think of the painting he was working on.

"I think we'd love it. Is it wheelchair accessible?"

"Mostly. The main floor is. We don't have the elevator installed yet for the loft, but I'll get it in next month, I hope."

"Well, then, I'll come and bring the kids. We all need a little culture in our lives, right?" She shook his hand. "I'll be back in touch with you about the house. I just need to finagle some numbers."

"No problem. You know how to reach me." He waited until Shyanne was rolling onto the van's platform to get into his car. When she was fully loaded and the door shut, he backed out of the driveway.

He might have found a buyer for the house!

Chapter Ten

"DO YOU NEED A HAND with that light?" Jonah asked.

Kaya looked down at him from the ladder, where she was adjusting the track lighting to focus on the painting she had hung earlier. Jonah had been giving her a crash course on all things gallery from his theory of design, lighting, pricing policies, and how he'd chosen the pieces. He'd been pleased at how quickly she'd picked things up.

"You can hold the ladder for me," she said. "I start to get a little nervous when I'm up here."

He shot her an apologetic look as he held one side. "I shouldn't be having you climb the ladder. It came from Gram's so it's probably from before Grandpa was in a wheelchair. That's been a while." He had stepped into the office to talk to one of his artists and left her to work on the section—he'd taken much longer than anticipated. He hadn't thought about the condition of the ladder, but he should have. He watched her tweak the light a little to the left so it hit the painting perfectly. "You're getting good at this." She had hung it all for great visual appeal and adjusted the series of lights.

"I'm a fast learner." Kaya started down the ladder.

She always seemed to have a positive attitude. "I ordered a couple of sandwiches. I was just going to run next door to pick them up. Are you ready for a break?"

She tucked her hair back behind one ear. "Sure. You don't have to provide lunch so often."

It wasn't that often, just a few times now. He hadn't expected her to pick up so many hours when she first showed up at his door, but she had been a lifesaver. "I know, but you're giving up so much time to work here this week—more than I ever expected. I appreciate it." He hadn't acted very appreciative the first day she'd shown up, but wanted to make up for it.

She descended the ladder and he stepped away, not wanting to crowd her. "I'll grab that food and meet you in the back in a few minutes." He hurried next door to pay for lunch and brought back two sandwiches and the best French fries he'd ever eaten. They were thick cut and beer battered, giving them twice the tastiness. Having them so close made giving up his favorite New York pizza far more bearable. "How is it you have so much time to help me, anyway? Don't you have a ton of clients?" Surely she didn't charge enough to pay all of her bills and feed the horses off of a couple of hours each day.

She shrugged while he unpacked the bag. "I'm busier when it's warmer. A lot of patients take a break during the worst of the winter because of the cold and bad roads. I'm not working for Kenworth's anymore, either."

He offered her the choice of ham or turkey and she took the ham. He split the fries with her, curious about that statement. "You were working at Kenworth's?" He remembered seeing her there, playing with the perfume bottles. Could she have been rearranging the display and not testing them all? "That day, when I saw you there?"

"Yeah. But last Monday..." She grimaced, and peeled back the sandwich wrapping. "Well, we'll just say I had scheduling conflicts, so I had to quit. I was only going to be there through the holiday season, anyway. I spent a good portion of the money I set aside to buy winter feed and to repair the barn roof, so I need a little extra to get my animals through the winter. I was glad when this opened up."

"The joys of home ownership," he said.

She fished out her water bottle. "Owning your own business has its drawbacks, too. I love it, don't get me wrong, but being responsible for every penny when there aren't a lot of extra ones can be tough sometimes. It's busy in the summer, so I save for the winter, but sometimes it doesn't all work out the way I plan."

"Tell me about it. I thought I had more than enough money to get this off the ground, but one thing or the next has been chipping away at my cushion. Don't worry, though. You'll get paid." Even if he had to live on Ramen and mac and cheese for a solid six months. He really hated cooking for himself.

She didn't look worried. "Good to hear. The horses don't really thrive on snow as their main food source."

"They're so picky." He smiled to let her know it was a joke. "You seem to visit Grams a lot."

"Yeah, she was so good to me when I moved into my grandma's a couple of years ago. Always there to offer a kind word or bring over dinner when I was exhausted from working hard fixing fences. She always tells me stories about my grandma. It helps keep her alive for me. Ora also talks a lot about her grandkids. You especially. She's very proud. I think it's great that you came back here to keep an eye on her."

Jonah picked at a piece of shredded lettuce on his sandwich. "I'd do anything for her. Besides, I love it here, and I was ready for a change. A complete change." He'd been dragging around trying to paint post-Janet. This was a fresh start in many ways.

"She said you haven't painted anything in a long time." Kaya's words were hesitant, as though she wanted to ask, but didn't want to pry.

"I hit a wall." He paused. It felt wrong to gloss it over with Kaya, though he didn't know why. He went with the impulse. "I was dating someone seriously. When it ended, I found I could only paint dark stuff. Stuff I wouldn't buy or hang, and definitely wouldn't sell. I tried working through it, but I tried so hard to paint things I wasn't feeling that I ended up not being able to paint at all. Nothing remotely good, anyway. Technically correct, but not emotionally true at all, so I had to stop. The gallery is sort of my backup plan." It had taken a long time for him to admit it was what he had to do.

"That seems to have changed."

"What do you mean?"

"I saw the painting of Shyanne this morning; it's nearly done, right? It's beautiful. It takes my breath away, actually."

He was pleased that she liked it. He'd been so worried about whether it was as good as he thought. "Sometimes a change of scenery can make all the difference." He was starting to think maybe it was *Kaya* that had made all the difference, but he wasn't ready to go there. He studied her as she ate. Maybe he wasn't as far off as he'd thought, though.

"Final delivery just came in." Jonah greeted Kaya when she arrived Wednesday morning. "I can't wait to see what Manuel sent me. He's an incredible artist. Makes me feel like a neophyte half the time. You, especially, will appreciate these."

Glad he didn't appear the least upset about the other man overshadowing him, Kaya followed him to the back room where the paintings were crated up. It was about time the shipment arrived. The delivery was several days late and they would open the gallery the next day for the grand gala. Jonah had been putting off setting up the last few things, wanting to make sure he got the placement exactly right. She still had a few small sculptures to uncrate as well that had been delivered the previous afternoon. As she walked through the gallery behind him, she saw the stands had been erected, so she should be able to get them all placed so they would be ready to open the next day.

Jonah picked up the crowbar from its usual location and pried the crate open, moving slowly and carefully, so he wouldn't damage anything inside. The wood groaned as the nails were pried out, and the smell of pine filled the air. She loved the scent, always had, but after three of these uncrating ceremonies, it was gaining a new significance. She'd learned how valuable everything was to him—not in money, though there was certainly that, but intrinsically, as a piece of someone's soul, as he had claimed one day. She didn't quite get it, as a few of the pieces looked like nonsense to her.

Not Jonah's paintings, though. They had always touched her somewhere deep inside, starting with the painting he had done of his grandparents in their backyard that hung in Ora's living room. That had been done when he was still a teen. It didn't have half the skill of the painting of Shyanne that she had seen waiting for a frame the previous night. She would have to invite Evelyn, give her a chance to at least see the painting before someone else snatched it up.

Kaya could hardly believe the grand opening was the next day. After she helped Jonah through the first week or so, he wouldn't need her anymore, and their time together would be over. She didn't think she could fade back into being just two people who lived in the same city. Not now. She watched him lift the first painting, which faced away from her, from the crate and his eyes lit up with pleasure.

If things worked out for the Shoemakers to buy Ora's house, then he wouldn't even have a reason to come to the neighborhood and maybe pop by to say hello. Could she let that happen? She didn't think so. Not without at least trying to see if something might develop between them. Something more.

She tried not to think about that right now. She needed to focus on the task at hand, she reminded herself. They had work to do. When he turned the stretched cotton canvas around so she could see the painting, the breath caught in her throat. The craggy rocks and vibrant green bushes practically leapt off the canvas, the details so minute it looked almost more like a photograph than a painting. But it was the chestnut bay standing near the center that really got her. She could almost feel the horse hair under her fingers, hear the horse blowing air through his nostrils.

Kaya took a step closer and lifted her hand, half expecting to feel hair on the canvas, but stopped before making contact and slid her hand into her pocket. "That's incredible." Even inches away, it barely looked like brush strokes, the acrylic paints were so masterfully mixed and applied.

"All of his paintings have this kind of detail. He amazes me. Give me a hand here?" Jonah carefully set the painting aside and reached for the next one.

Blinking to overcome the stunned sensation she felt, Kaya cleared away some space on his framing counter and removed a smaller painting from the crate. It didn't feature a horse, but was equally as detailed.

In all, there were five paintings, each as wonderful as the first, and four of them featured horses. The one featuring a palomino grabbed her by the throat, and she wished she had the money to purchase the four-figure painting. That wasn't going to happen, though.

They set up the last few statues, found places for the remaining paintings, and Kaya helped Jonah decide on frames for Manuel's paintings.

"Some of the other paintings here don't have frames," she pointed out. "Why are you framing all of these?"

"They'll show better with frames, and that velvet mat for this one," he gestured to the first one he had uncrated. "I actually have a buyer in mind to look at them. I'm sure he'll buy at least a couple."

"That would be fantastic for you." She leaned back against the framing counter, her hands wrapped around the carpeted surface. "Will you have time to finish the frames before the show tomorrow night?" She knew they were pushing the deadline to the max and he had some of the artists and community elite coming for a thank-you lunch in the afternoon, followed by the general grand opening for the public in the evening. Thursdays were her only afternoon off so she'd be there most of the day.

"Yeah, if I ignore the phone for a few hours this afternoon, it shouldn't be a problem." He ran his fingers along the edge, near her hand. "I appre-ciate your help."

"It's been a pleasure seeing this all come together." More than that, really; she hated to see this end.

"You've been great to work with. Seriously, I don't think I could have managed it without you. Not with an ounce of sanity left." Jonah's finger's tapped lightly in the wooden backing. "I know you need to get back to your animals soon, but I wondered if you could break away for a while tonight. For dinner."

"Like a thank-you dinner?" Kaya wasn't sure what his expectations were. She hoped he saw it as a date—that he wanted it as much as she did, but she had never been good at reading him.

He watched her face carefully. "Actually, like a date. I've enjoyed getting to know you. I wondered what it would be like to spend time together away from here."

She grinned, relieved that he might have feelings for her. "I think I'd like that. What did you have in mind?" Her thoughts were already racing, trying to figure out what to wear—she hadn't exactly had the opportunity to dress up for him yet. Of course, she would be in much nicer clothes for the opening celebration.

He picked up her hand and gave her fingers a light squeeze. "When was the last time you went ice skating?"

Kaya blinked, taken totally by surprise. She'd been thinking of something a little more formal. Ice skating was definitely not formal. Not even a little bit. "A long time, at least not since college, maybe not since high school."

His expression made her wonder if he was pleased he set her a little off-kilter. "I haven't been out this season, but I used to skate a lot. Do you have a pair of skates?"

"I think so. If not, I could probably borrow some from someone. I know several of my neighbors ice skate." Flo, who lived two doors down, took her kids out skating a lot and their feet might be the same size. Or Laurie around the corner.

Jonah grinned, happier and more relaxed than she'd seen him before. "Great. I'll take care of dinner. You want to meet me at the lake at seven? That will give you time to milk the goats and settle everyone in for the night, and time for me to get a fair amount of framing out of the way."

He wasn't picking her up, either? This wasn't seeming all that date-ish right now. "I could do that." Chickadee Lake was kitty-corner across the street from the gallery and surrounded by trees and picnic tables. "I should go then, take care of things back home." Search for those skates. "See you tonight."

"See you." Jonah's lips turned up and he watched her grab her coat and walk out.

As she drove back around to the front of the building, she saw Keira Kenworth directing people to set up for the Carol Fest in the plaza across the street from the Gallery. She was sorry she would have to miss it that afternoon. She remembered going to one as a kid and the sweetness of cider and donuts on her tongue. It would be over before her date with Jonah that night.

Her thoughts turned back to Jonah. He was usually a little uptight, which could easily be because of his work. Kaya looked forward to seeing him in a more casual setting and hoped it didn't turn into a disaster.

Chapter Eleven

IT HAD BEEN A LONG TIME since Kaya had been to Chickadee Lake. The city allowed non-motorized boats on it in the summer, and cleared the ice for skating for a couple months during the winter—depending on the weather. Thanks to several weeks of sub-zero temperatures at night, it was fully frozen now.

Kaya found her old skates in a musty wooden box in the attic and checked them over. They were worn—she'd had them since she was fifteen and had bought them second-hand to begin with. But they were still just fine for another use. She pulled on a second set of warm socks and crammed her feet back into her boots. Extra insulation would be much appreciated once she got on the ice.

Though she told herself it didn't matter, Kaya debated for more than ten minutes over her collection of scarves and hats before finalizing her outfit with an ultra-soft navy yarn set Ora had given her the previous Christmas.

Why was she so worried about what she wore? Jonah had seen her in her coveralls, for goodness sake, with her hair pulled up, sweat dripping from her face, and stinking of horse droppings. So what was the deal now?

Kaya admitted to herself that she liked Jonah more than she had thought possible. Things were going so well and she wondered if this was the start of something really terrific or if it would be just one more disappointment in the dating department.

She went out to her vehicle and climbed in, hoping the clouds that were rolling in would hold off on dumping a new layer of snow long enough for them to have a nice evening. A cloud cover might raise the temperature a few degrees, though, if there wasn't too much wind—that would be appreciated since the night was already in the teens and dropping.

Kaya found a parking spot behind the art gallery and walked over to the pond—there was parking on the side of the road, but with all of the snow they'd had lately, it would be half-full of snow drifts and her truck had a long bed, so it would stick into the road. There were already plenty of people skating, flashing in and out of the well-lit areas. Not only did the seasonal spotlights illuminate the cleared area, but the colored twinkle lights that brightened several of the trees nearby helped make it easier to see everything. It looked almost magical.

"Hey," Jonah said, coming up behind Kaya. "You want to eat first while the food's hot? We can grab some hot cocoa at Fay's Café after. She makes the best on the planet." Jonah was bundled in his heavy winter coat, a red, knit scarf double-knotted at his neck.

It looked a lot like Kaya's scarf and she wondered how many other scarves Ora had made. "Dinner sounds good. I'm freezing already."

"Sorry about the cold date, it's the one downside of ice skating." He led her over to one of the picnic benches and started setting out cartons. There were two deep bowls of chicken noodle soup, hunks of bread, warm, spiced cider, and gingerbread cookies.

"Looks delicious. Is this also from the café?" Kaya had only been there once, when she had been a child still. Her grandpa had taken her in during one of her visits.

"Yes. It's nice it's so close to the gallery. I've been eating there a lot lately." He passed over a spoon and took a seat on the freezing bench.

"Nice this table happened to be clear." She noticed the others were all covered in more than a foot of snow.

"I cleared it off before picking up the soup," he admitted. "I figured eating standing up wouldn't be much fun."

"The window display at the gallery looks great. I can't wait for opening night," Kaya could see the gallery from her seat, though it was far enough away that she couldn't read anything on the windows. The lighting hit the paintings just right, and the sculpture near the front window would catch anyone's eye. Cars rushed past as people hurried to their next holiday event. He had a prime location.

"I had a call today, someone who saw the sculpture as they walked by. They wanted to buy it. We talked price and they said they'll come by tomorrow during the opening for a closer look." He appeared very pleased with himself.

"That's a good omen, to have interest before you're even opened."

"I hope so. I feel like I've put all of my eggs in this one basket and I'm kinda terrified that it'll bust." He played with a chunk of his bread. "I don't know what my next move would be."

That was a moment of honesty and vulnerability Kaya couldn't ignore. She hoped that meant he was open to talk. She decided to start with something easy. "How long have you been drawing?"

He smiled, countering with, "How young do most kids pick up a pencil?"

"So pretty much always. Fair enough." She took a spoonful of the sinfully delicious chicken noodle soup and asked another way. "When did it go from, hey, this is fun, to hey, this is what I want to do with my life?"

"I can't remember not loving to draw, and according to my mom, painting came right at its heels. I think I was five when my kindergarten class went on a field trip to a museum. I saw these huge, amazing paintings and thought, hey, this art thing, it could be something. That's what I want to do when I grow up." He grinned. "I went home and started drawing on the wall, planning a mural."

That made her chuckle; she could imagine it perfectly. "What did your mom think about that?"

"After she got over the pencil marks on everything, she reconsidered and agreed to let me paint the walls. She even bought me some paints to do everything. I started mixing different shades and splashing things up there. It was really terrible." He grinned at her before taking a large bite of bread.

"But you had fun?"

"Yeah." He chewed and swallowed. "I had a lot of fun. Mom took a bunch of pictures, proud as can be, and gave me a serious artist's sketch pad. I thought I was the king of the art world. I started taking art lessons through a summer program, and kept drawing. In third grade we expanded the mural to a second wall and it was somewhat less horrible. But not much."

"And then you learned more, practiced more, and covered wall number three?" Kaya could see where this was going.

"Of course. By the time I graduated from high school, the mural had all been repainted with a new scene, some of it twice over, and each wall was significantly better than the one before. I also had a large portfolio of sketches and a reasonable, pretty decent, collection of paintings. That got me a scholarship." He said it as if it were a matter of course instead of a major accomplishment, though she didn't imagine he'd been nearly as casual about it at the time.

"When did you decide you wanted to use mostly watercolor instead of the other kinds of paint? Has it always been your thing?" She knew a few other people who were artists of varying quality, and though they all did different things, few worked in several mediums.

Jonah finished his soup and picked up one of the gingerbread cookies. "I dabbled in all of them. In college I spent a lot of time learning pastels, oils, acrylics, and watercolor. I'm reasonably proficient in all of them—not spectacular, but reasonably proficient. The challenge of watercolor really stuck with me."

"Why is it more of a challenge than the others?" Kaya loved the way his expression opened up and his face became animated when he talked about art. She had asked a lot of extra questions about the pieces displayed in the gallery as well, happy to see his enthusiasm. There was satisfaction mixed in with his enthusiasm now, which she found extra enticing.

"If you mess up with acrylics or oil, you can paint over it. Start again. Worst case scenario, you have to add a couple layers of paint to cover up the mistake. With watercolor, you can go darker, but you can't go lighter. I have to block off white space and be extra careful because I can't undo something once the color is on the paper."

She hadn't thought of that before, but she could see that it would keep a lot of artists from choosing watercolor. "I think I would be intimidated by that, not being able to fix it."

"It just means being more creative."

"Don't you still work with oils sometimes? I've seen a couple at Ora's. She always brags on you."

"There's something to be said for the smear of paint, and the sensation of building it up, a layer at a time. It's a different kind of work, but I enjoy it just as much, in its own way. You can add physical texture to the painting in oil, which is nice for certain projects. It works well for dramatic or emotional pieces. I don't use it often, but sometimes when I'm in the mood." He played with the end of his cookie, pensive, then looked back at her.

Kaya paused for a moment, not wanting to push, but he seemed open so she broached the topic that had been burning in the back of her mind. "You said you stopped painting after things ended with a previous relationship? It must have been very serious." She wanted to ask outright about what happened, dying to know if his heart was still broken or if he was really feeling better. This was the best she could do, though.

He finished his cookie, studying her face, then washed it down with the end of his cider. "I was dating someone. Seriously. We were talking marriage and were excited for the future. I had this big show at a major gallery, my career was taking off, and everything seemed so perfect. The night my big show opened, she was supposed to meet me at the gallery. We'd had a little argument that afternoon, but I thought we had worked it out. She never showed up."

He stared at his hands and pain etched around his eyes and along his forehead. "I remember being so angry that she had flaked out and missed my big night, that she hadn't really let go of our argument like she said she had. It turned out she was in an accident on her way to the opening. I never got to talk to her again."

"Oh my." Kaya didn't know what to say about that. She reached out and took his hand in hers.

He squeezed back. "It messed me up for a long time. I wondered if it was my fault. I was mad at myself for being mad at her instead of worrying about her. I hadn't known about the accident, but for a long time I thought I should have known. Like a better attitude on my part would have changed the situation. I just wanted everything to be different. That was nearly two years ago, and I couldn't paint for a long time. When I did, it was awful, really—so uninspired. I was doing better work in high school—not technically better, but emotionally better work. The stuff from my showing sold pretty well, but after a while I realized I wasn't producing anything sellable, and didn't know if I ever would again. That's when I bought the gallery and fixed it up."

"Because you couldn't stand to not be around art, even if you were having trouble creating it yourself?" Kaya had seen the joy and excitement in his eyes as he uncrated paintings and unwrapped statues. She understood that excitement and zeal.

"Exactly."

"But that painting of Shyanne, it's amazing. And the one of Chad on the horse, I'm sure it's not recognizable to someone who doesn't know him well, but it's him, right?"

He smiled, threading their fingers together. "Yeah. I couldn't help it, though it made me think of seeing you going for a ride when you were Shyanne's age, and calling back to your grandma that you were doing it."

Kaya chuckled. "Sounds about right. I always loved horses, for as long as I can remember. Being able to work with them every day is like a dream come true."

"Then we both got our dreams, in one way or another." By now he had both of her hands held tightly in his. "We should probably start skating before we turn into popsicles."

"Good idea." They started cleaning up the empty containers.

"Have you thought about teaching art classes up here? Maybe in the summer, like the ones you took?" Kaya had wondered if there were any good classes in the area. After working with him, she might be interested in one, just to learn more about it.

"I'm not a teacher." He didn't even give the question a moment's thought.

"Why not?"

"Because, I'm an artist, not a teacher."

It irritated her a little that he wouldn't even consider it. "But you probably thought you weren't a gallery owner once too, didn't you? And now you are. So why not expand that a little more? I didn't know I wanted to help other people with horses, not for a long time. It took nearly finishing my degree, planning to become a vet, before I even started to consider therapy."

He pursued that line of discussion instead of the one she'd been asking about. "Do you wish you had taken more vet training?"

She considered calling him on the change of topic, but decided to let it go. "I got in a few basic classes. I do a lot of the regular maintenance on my animals since it's far less expensive than bringing in a vet, but therapy is where I shine. It's what makes it all worthwhile."

Jonah handed her a pair of skates. "I can tell that it's important to you. I'm glad. Everyone should have the opportunity to do work that they love. I wish more people did."

"More people could if they prioritized. You didn't become a great artist by sitting at home and wishing for more. The gallery isn't happening because you long for a reason to be near your grandma, it's happening because you dug in and got to work. Nothing really great, really worthwhile, happens without hard work."

"I guess that's true." A storm was moving in and snow was on the forecast for the night, but the cloud cover didn't seem to have warmed the air much. "Do you think it will start to snow before we go home tonight?"

"I hope so. I think skating under a light snow would be cool." And romantic, a draw she couldn't ignore.

They sat on a bench near the lake to put on their skates. "Have you skated much?" Jonah gave his laces a final tug and tied a bow.

"I've been out a few times over the years, but not recently." It made her a little nervous. What if she made a fool of herself?

He grinned at her. "If you did okay last time, you should be fine tonight, once you get the hang of it again." He stood to face her, giving her a hand up.

Jonah tucked their boots under the bench and he took her hand as they crossed the sidewalk and made their way down the ramp to the ice.

She had to stiffen her ankles to stand. Her skate blades sank into the snow as they crossed to the ice. "I hope so. They say it's like riding a bike, you never forget how."

Kaya was wobbly at first, needing a minute to get the hang of it again. Jonah took off as if he had been on skates every day of his life. "You don't seem to be rusty." She wasn't sure if she admired his grace or resented it.

He circled back to take her hand. "I love to skate, summer or winter, if I get tied up in knots and can't paint, I'll grab my in-line skates or ice skates and go out for a while. It usually helps me work through whatever's on my mind and gives me a chance to look for inspiration."

"In that case, it's a good thing you have Chickadee Lake." Kaya wondered how much time he'd spent skating after his girlfriend's accident, or if he had been too upset.

"Looks like you still need a minute to get your feet." His hand was surprisingly warm considering how cold it was outside.

A trio of boys whizzed by them and another couple skated leisurely around the edges. One little girl was trying a sit-spin near the middle of the pond, but fell over. She frowned, pushed herself back up and tried again.

Kaya admired her fortitude. "I've never tried anything like that. She must be pretty determined."

"You don't become an Olympic ice skater by zooming around the edges," Jonah said, approval filling his voice. If he had noticed that she was steady now and didn't need him to hold her hand, he didn't indicate it. She wasn't about to pull away.

How was it that even through their gloves, she felt a bit of electricity when they touched? She tried to ignore the feeling and enjoy the exercise.

He turned, ending up in front of her, skating backward. "Have you ever tried any kind of turns or special maneuvers?"

"I've skated backward a couple of times. Badly. I always fell."

"Try it now, come on." He glanced behind him, then gave her hand a tug.

"Okay, but you need to keep an eye out behind us. I don't want to end up in a heap on the edge of the ice." She really didn't trust herself.

"Don't worry, I've got this." He gave her hand a tug again and she took a fortifying breath before turning into his arms so her back was facing his front. She could do this.

He released her hand and put one hand on each side of her waist so he could guide her backward. "Good. Just make your feet open and close, pushing the ice. Now, turn again to face me."

She started to twist and the tip of her skate caught the ice. He managed to keep her from totally falling, but only just. His knee hit the ice instead.

Kaya cringed. "Oh, I'm sorry. Did that hurt?" She could just see herself seriously injuring him on their first date.

65

He stood up again and took her hand. "It barely brushed the ice, it's fine. Try again. Come on." He started them moving again. When she was doing well with that, he released her for a moment, twirling twice as he moved across the ice, then took her hand again. "You can do that. It's pretty simple."

Yes, but she'd learned long ago that simple didn't always mean easy. "I don't know."

"Just try. Watch my feet." He demonstrated again, pointing out his technique, then urged her on. They laughed together, moved through the motions and she fell on her butt a few times before she managed it even once.

Kaya threw her arms around his neck in celebration. "I can't believe I did it!"

"I can. You just had to keep trying." His arms slid around her waist, pulling her closer.

Their faces were only inches apart and Kaya realized he was going to kiss her. Maybe. And that she wanted him to. A lot. She looked up into his eyes and the icy air caught in her throat. She pressed her lips together, and his gaze dropped to her mouth.

The trio of rowdy boys passed them again, a little too close for comfort and laughing loudly. One of them made a crude comment about the two of them.

It broke the spell and Jonah pulled back. "I'm half frozen. You ready for that hot cocoa?"

Part of Kaya didn't want it to end, but her teeth were chattering and she knew she needed to get inside before she froze something important. "Sounds good."

He took her hand again, and led her to the bench to change back into their boots. The boots were freezing, but Kaya told herself they would warm up quickly in the café. She tied the skate laces together and set them over her shoulder, then took the hand Jonah offered her. She felt a little giddy that it seemed second nature to walk hand-in-hand with him and then thought maybe it had been a little too long since she was in a relationship. The sidewalks were clear and ice free, so it wasn't as if she needed help, but she wasn't about to complain.

"Did your parents have horses?" Jonah asked as they waited for the light to change so they could cross the street.

"No, my Dad died when I was young and Mom and I lived in a little apartment. There was no room or money for horses. I loved whenever we came to Grandma's, because she taught me to ride when I was so young, and she always let me spend as much time with the horses as I wanted."

"I didn't know that about your dad. I'm sorry, it must have been hard."

She just nodded. It wasn't something she wanted to discuss in depth on the first date.

"I remember you, a couple of times. I think. When I visited Grams."

That pleased her, though it shouldn't have mattered. "That's possible. After my dad died and Mom was struggling just to pay the bills, I spent a lot of school breaks with Grandma, mostly because Mom couldn't afford daycare, I think. I didn't complain. I love it here. This town, the farm, the animals. The Candy Counter at Kenworth's."

Kaya was pleased when he chuckled at that. She finished her line of thought. "I loved Grandma most of all. She made me feel safe and loved."

The light changed and they were prompted to cross the street. "You didn't feel safe at home?"

Had she said that? No, but he wasn't entirely wrong, either—though not because her mom wasn't great, when she had time to breathe and actually talk with Kaya. "We couldn't afford much, and I didn't go out when Mom wasn't there, especially when I was younger. She worked all the time, or it seemed that way, so after school I came home and locked myself in the apartment. I knew bad things were going on in the neighborhood; we even had a few drive-by shootings in the area, so I stayed home after school until I was in high school. Even then, if it hadn't been for Robbin, my best friend, I wouldn't have gotten out much. I was really shy."

"I don't see much of that now." They passed the front windows of the gallery, headed for the café beyond it.

"I've gotten over a lot of the shyness. When I'm having trouble with it, I usually brazen through. It's not always easy and I don't always succeed."

Jonah studied her for a few seconds, his expression soft. "Well, you make it look easy."

"Thanks." It had taken a long time to at least give off the appearance of confidence in public. She wasn't always sure she managed it.

They walked into Fay's Café and were instantly enveloped by smells of hamburgers, coffee, and the sweet tinge of ice cream in the air. The style was classic 50s—it had definitely been updated recently. It still sported the white enameled tables with silver trim on the sides, plush booths with matching black Naugahyde, and white and black tiled floors, but they were a lot shinier than she remembered. Pen and ink sketches of girls in poodle skirts and roller skates, kids dancing in front of a juke box and similar scenes graced the walls. The twenty-something waitress who came over to the table they had chosen didn't look like she had come from the fifties, though. Her long, wavy hair was dyed black with hot pink streaks, she wore a snug T-shirt over frayed jeans, almost as much jewelry as Mr. T, and her arms were covered in tats. When she greeted them, her voice was soft and sweet, like you'd expect to hear from a southern belle, only without the accent. "Hello, how are we doing tonight?" She looked at Kaya. "You work for him, right? I've seen you coming and going a few times."

"Yes, Kaya Fiedler. I live in town, but I don't get out much. I haven't been here in years."

"I'm Fay Griffith, and I hope you make it back again soon. What can I get for you two? You look cold."

Kaya was stymied. This young woman was Fay?

"We are cold. Could we get two hot cocoas with extra whipped cream?" Jonah asked.

She grinned as she made a note. "You do like your whipped cream."

"I love your cocoa, and the whipped cream makes it extra special. It's the best cocoa I've ever had."

"Flattery *will* get you that extra whipped cream. Anything else?"

"Not tonight, thanks," Jonah said.

She scribbled something on her notepad and slipped it back into her pocket as she walked away.

"You really haven't been here in years?" Jonah asked. "They have the best hamburgers, and their onion rings are to die for."

"Why do I get the feeling that you eat here a lot?"

"Because you're observant. With the gallery next door, I eat here at least once per day." Their hands had separated as they had divested themselves of skates and coats before they took their booth, but now he captured hers from the tabletop again. "You've been so much help getting the gallery ready. I don't think I'd be ready for tomorrow's opening without you. Even if I'd given up sleeping altogether."

She shook her head in disagreement. "I haven't worked that many hours. I wish I could have helped more."

"I appreciate it. I see how busy you've been. It was lucky for me that you had scheduling problems at Kenworth's. Are you sure you don't want to keep working for me after the holidays?"

She shared his smile, glad he liked having her around. "It's tempting, but I've earned enough for my animal feed, and I need to get back to all of the things I've been putting off on the farm." Though she had no interest in working two jobs permanently, she would miss spending so much time with him. "Hasn't this always been Fay's? How is that possible when she's so young?"

"Her grandmother owned it before. She died a couple of years back and Fay, who was named after her grandma, stepped in and took over. She totally redid the place. Do you like it?"

"It's fantastic, seriously. I love the art around the walls. Is that new too?"

He looked up at the pen and ink drawing nearest to them. "I don't remember them, but I didn't come here much when I was growing up. We weren't in town all that often. Maybe I didn't notice them back then. They're really good."

The conversation continued, easy and fun for the rest of the evening, before they walked back to the gallery to double-check a couple of last-minute things for the night.

"I should head out. Five-o'clock milking comes early," Kaya said when they approached the front door.

He veered toward her car. "It was a nice evening. Thanks for joining me." He took her hand once more, giving it a light squeeze.

She smiled, unable to do anything else. "Thanks for asking. It's been a really long time since I had such a fun date." She didn't want to leave. Being with him made her heart race, her stomach quiver, and her nerves stand on end.

Or maybe that last one was the freezing cold breeze that wrapped around them.

"I'll see you in the morning? We have a few odds and ends that need to be done before the artist and dignitary lunch tomorrow." He stepped in a little closer to her.

"You bet. I don't have any clients, so I'm yours all day."

His eyes never left her face as they shifted closer together. "Is it stupid that I'm so nervous? I've been to so many galleries and opening night shows. I know what I'm doing."

"It's not stupid at all. This is *your* gallery. You're bound to have butterflies." She sure did. Right now.

He shifted even closer, and she met him halfway. "You seem like the kind of person who likes butterflies."

"What can I say, like calls to like, and apparently I'm a bit of a flutter-budget."

"You don't seem flighty to me." They stood there, together for several aching seconds, the light breeze blowing hair across her face. He lifted a hand to brush the hair away. "You amaze me." His lips pressed against hers and she felt sweet excitement fill her chest. Finally. She wrapped her free arm around his neck and pulled him closer, deepening the kiss for one glorious moment before he started to pull back.

She released him and he backed away several inches. Jonah studied her face for a moment before letting go of her other hand, which he still held. "See you in the morning?"

"Yeah. Bright and early." Kaya clicked the door open with her remote. He opened the door for her and helped her inside. For a moment, she thought maybe he was going to say something else, but after a moment's pause, he shut the door, and waved as she drove away.

He watched her until she drove around a corner and she couldn't see him anymore.

Kaya's heart was pounding and she could hardly believe the excitement that thrummed in her veins. It had been such a good night.

She hoped he felt the same.

Chapter Twelve

JONAH WATCHED UNTIL KAYA was out of sight, then turned back to his gallery. He had finished making the frames for Manuel's last few paintings that afternoon while Kaya had been working with clients. He just needed to assemble all of the pieces and seal the paintings against humidity and other things that could degrade them over time.

He went in the back way and finished assembling the frames. It was getting late, but his fingers itched. He just wasn't sure what he wanted to work on. He had framed the painting of Shyanne, as well as the charcoal sketch of Chad on horseback. That one was shot from the side, with just a hint of Chad's face silhouetted against the darkness behind him, the lights on the barn and a couple of poles around the ring lighting him up. It would be nice to have a couple pieces of his own to add to the collection. Especially something new.

He took the last couple of paintings out and hung them in the spaces he and Kaya had selected for them and then stood in the front window.

The lake was empty now, the fifteen or twenty people who had been there earlier had no doubt escaped the cold for warm beds. A glance at his watch told him it was nearly eleven, but he couldn't settle down.

After Janet had died, he hadn't even wanted to get involved in another relationship. The pain had been following him for over a year, an ache that persisted, even when he was involved in something else. He had gone on a test date with another woman a couple of months before moving to Echo Ridge, but that had been an unqualified disaster and he hadn't tried again since.

Kaya, though, had, well... not *tiptoed* her way into his life. More like barreled in full-steam ahead. He hadn't been able to keep her at arm's length, despite being blown away by how pretty she was the first time he'd seen her over the fence.

Her dark beauty made his breath catch. Maybe that was why he had been so gruff with her in the store. And again about the chicken therapy. Actually, he still thought that one was odd.

He was such an idiot sometimes. He had never thought he would find someone else he could care about as much as Janet, but maybe there was something going on with Kaya, something that could last.

The extra lights over the lake turned off. It was eleven, Jonah noted. They must have been on a timer. The clouds moved then and the full moon, just setting over the mountain, broke through them, shining down on the lake. Illuminating it again.

When he had asked Kaya out, he thought maybe an evening away from work would break him from the spell he seemed to be under— surely the date would be awful, and then he wouldn't wonder anymore. But it hadn't been awful. It had been perfect.

She was willing to try new things, didn't whine about the cold, asked about him and actually paid attention to what he said. She shared private things about herself as well. And the kiss—it had blown him away. It was only supposed to be a peck, a light salute to a nice night, but when she had reciprocated he had been caught. He hadn't wanted to let go.

He found himself, as he had assembled the frames that night, thinking of ways to convince her to keep working for him, at least once in a while, to have her around. It hadn't really been that long since he'd had a new relationship, had it?

He double-checked the front door lock, though he didn't think they'd opened it that day, and headed back to his work room. A fresh sheet of paper and some charcoal were at hand and he started sketching her that night, on the ice, laughing and twirling. The sketch was quick and had its own beauty, but it wasn't exactly what he was going for. He realized he needed to try again, and pulled out a fresh sheet, opening his pastel pencils, to try again. This time he was considerably happier with the result.

Chapter Thirteen

JITTERS WOULDN'T LEAVE JONAH'S SYSTEM. He'd been awake since five o'clock, after being up until nearly one drawing. He was tired, but didn't think he would have been able to sleep, even if he hadn't been expecting Kaya to arrive any minute. She'd been at work at eight on the dot every morning since she started working for him—surely she wouldn't stop that now.

Unless she had thought twice about how things had ended between them the previous night. Would it make things awkward? He hoped not.

A knock came from the front door and he walked over to open it. It was Fay. "I brought over your order."

"You didn't have to do that." Jonah took the other end of the rolling stainless steel cart she had used to carry the selection of pastries, cookies, and cupcakes he had ordered for the day's events.

"I brought in extra help for this morning so I could finish up your order—and I hoped to get a quick peek at your gallery. I'll be totally swamped all day, and possibly into the evening." She looked over his shoulder into the depths of the room.

"When someone provides me with such excellent service, I can't say no."

She picked up a white fast food sack from the cart and handed it to him. "I figured you wouldn't take time to eat breakfast, so I brought over a couple of breakfast sandwiches for you and Kaya; as a grand opening present from me."

"Wow, thanks, that's really nice. No wonder Fay's is my favorite place to eat."

"You *are* my best customer. Do you mind if I wander for the three minutes I dare stay away?"

"You need to get some extra help there so you can get away once in a while. I don't think I've ever been in your café when you weren't there."

"Those are the pains of owning a business. Refurbishing the café was more than I bargained for." She didn't take her eyes off the art as she talked, walking slowly as she absorbed everything around her. "Most of the time I don't mind, but it would be nice to take time off sometimes."

Fay came to a stop in front of a pastel drawing of a young girl feeding pigeons in the park. She stared at it, totally engrossed. "This is amazing. Doesn't it just grab you by the throat?"

"The artist is very talented. I found her doing quick sketches of people for money in downtown New York. I asked about some of her other work and she promised to send me pictures of some of them. She planned a few more and here we are."

Corra was one of the few people Jonah had paid up front, taking a risk that some of her things might not sell quickly. She was so talented, but she couldn't keep doing the higher-quality work he needed without the financial help. He loved her pastels of people, mothers and babies, old couples sitting on park benches, children playing in the water. He knew she could be successful with her art if she kept at it.

When he got them in the mail, he'd put the drawings on his scanner. Part of his art deal with her was the ability to sell prints. He hadn't had time to print and mat them yet, but that was his next priority. "I'll have prints of that one in a week or so if you're interested."

"Totally. Let me know when it's ready and I'll come in for one."

"I noticed you have a nice collection of art at the diner. Anyone local?"

"Very local," she brightened. "Do you really like them?"

His brows furrowed and he heard a knock at the back door. "Did *you* draw them?"

"Yes."

He pointed at her as he headed for the back door. "We need to talk. I'll come take a closer look when I get a chance to breathe."

"Really?" Her voice rose in surprise.

He used the peep hole to check before opening the door, then let in Kaya. He blinked a couple of times when her long, wool coat was removed to reveal a green cowl-neck sweater in some soft fiber and a flowing skirt that twisted around her knees, leaving a long expanse of lower leg exposed. "Wow. You look great." He took the coat from her.

"Thanks. I'm glad you approve." She leaned in and dropped a quick peck on his lips, then walked on past him.

So much for awkwardness when she arrived. Jonah followed behind her, ducking into the workroom to hang up her coat and take a deep breath. He'd always thought she was pretty, but in that outfit she was nearly heart stopping.

"Those look good," Kaya was saying as Jonah entered the main room of the gallery a moment later. She was peeking in the boxes of desserts.

"Wait until you taste them." Fay said, glancing over her shoulder from across the room. "I had this Italian neighbor who taught me how to make them. You'll die, they're so good." Fay was not the least humble about her culinary talents.

"And I thought you just made burgers and gourmet hot chocolate." Kaya's voice held a slight hint of accusation.

"You have so much to learn. You must stop in more often." With a reluctant glance at the painting in front of her, Fay came back to the cart, and moved the last box to the long counter beside the front computer. She buttoned up her coat again. "I have to get back before Noland runs people out, but I'll come to look at the rest of your gallery another day."

"I'll be by to see your collection too," Jonah promised her. He didn't have time right away, but he couldn't wait to take a closer look. He'd been impressed with what he'd seen so far, and he wanted to highlight local artists.

Fay waved goodbye and whisked out the front door, making it ding behind her. Jonah locked the door behind her again.

"What was that all about?" Kaya asked.

"Apparently the art in the café is hers."

Kaya's eyes widened. "Wow. It's really good."

"Yes, it is." Jonah picked up the sack of breakfast sandwiches. "She brought us some sustenance. Maybe you aren't hungry now, though?" He withdrew the first egg, bacon and cheese sandwich, opening it so she could look it over.

She sniffed and smiled. "It *has* been a long time since breakfast. The goats demanded to be milked two hours ago."

He grinned and passed it over so he could fish out the other one for himself. The sandwich was spicy and cheesy and perfect in every way imaginable. There was no question that Fay was an artist.

"Oh my goodness. This is amazing." Kaya took a napkin to wipe her mouth while she chewed. "I definitely need to eat there sometimes."

"If you think this is good, you should try the breakfast platter."

They rhapsodized over their favorite foods while they finished their sandwiches, then got down to business. Jonah had printed tags for each of the artworks after he'd woken up early that morning, so they set them up, and took care of the food, as well as the dozens of other little details that seemed to crop up at the last moment.

Though there were still a few items Jonah wished he had taken care of when they officially opened their doors at eleven, he was pretty pleased with what they had accomplished.

When the mayor and his wife walked in a few minutes later, he greeted them with a smile and introduced himself. This was it.

At first the arrivals came like a trickle, then a stream. Not all of

Jonah's artists were able to come to the opening, but Corra showed up, her latest boyfriend in tow. She saw one of her pictures set up in the first alcove and stopped to stare. "I can't believe it's true. I kept thinking all of the way up here that I would arrive and find nothing of mine here, that it was all too good to be true."

"You did it, babe." The tall, angular guy by her side leaned over and kissed her cheek, then wandered off, muttering something about food.

Jonah wanted to snap at him that this was a big deal for an artist. Huge. Corra deserved more than a dismissive congratulations. Though he was irritated with the boyfriend, he let it go. It was her life. "Your new work is even better than the stuff I saw before. This one was particularly amazing. I feel privileged to be the first to show your art." When she beamed at him, he continued. "I've gotten several nice compliments on your work already today. Come on in and meet some of the other people." He took her by the elbow and steered her further into the gallery.

Corra's eyes were bright with excitement and interest and she paused to study several pieces for a moment before he hurried her on.

Other artists arrived and Jonah did his best to introduce them all around and make sure they met Kaya, in case they needed anything during their visit. He mingled and chatted, and made sure everyone was having a great time. He noticed Kaya doing the same, looking as utterly at home in her classy outfit as she had in mud boots and coveralls a few days earlier. She had a natural grace and ability to blend with all different types of people. If she was feeling uncomfortable or shy now, she wasn't showing it. Between talking to various people, she had used the computer to take payments for several of the artworks already.

When things were winding down and the local dignitaries were filtering out, Jonah came to stand beside Kaya. "I wondered how you would handle the crowd with your alleged shyness, but you handled it fine."

"I didn't feel like I handled it fine all of the time, but I don't think I made too big of a fool of myself. That will have to do." One corner of her mouth lifted in a wry smile.

"I don't think you did anything even remotely foolish. You looked perfectly at ease the whole time."

"Well, thank you."

The city manager stopped to compliment Jonah before leaving and Kaya wandered off to talk to Corra, who was taking her time walking through the gallery and checking out all of the displays. A few of them had sold tags on them already—including two of hers. He had promised her a bonus for anything that sold the first week. Her boyfriend was sitting on a bench off to the side, playing on his phone. At least he wasn't acting impatient and dragging her away before she was ready.

Eventually even Corra left and Jonah met Kaya by the computer. "How much did we sell?"

"Six pieces, with definite interest on three others. Not terrible considering half of the people here today were starving artists." She grinned at him. "Looks like you'll be paying some commissions and some bills."

"That's music to my ears." He stretched a little—his back was killing him. As were his feet. "Did you eat enough?"

"Hardly anything. Every time I thought about tasting something someone would come over and ask me questions."

"Great, let's sit and have a real meal." They cleaned up the remaining food from the lunch and took it into the back room, making sure to keep the door propped open so they could hear the front bell if someone came in.

"Corra's adorable," Kaya said when they were seated with a selection of the leftovers in front of them. "So excited, energetic, and fun. It kind of surprised me that her work has such depth and emotion. Just a stereotype, I guess."

"She was extra excited because of the show today. Usually she's a little more reserved. I get the feeling she's been through a lot." He took a bite of his meat-stuffed roll and chewed, watching her daintily handle the pineapple chunks on her fork.

"So what do we do about the empty spots in the gallery displays? Do you have some items to replace them with, or do we leave the sold sign and empty spot?"

"I have a few things I couldn't fit out there to fill what's actually been taken already. The items I'll be delivering will stay where they are for now."

"I noticed there's no price tag on the painting of Shyanne."

"If her mom buys the house, I figured I'd give it to her as a housewarming gift. If not, I thought I'd offer it to her for sale first. Most moms would want that chance."

Kaya stared at him, a slight smile on her lips, surprise in her eyes. "That's very sweet."

"That's me, I'm sweet." He managed not to roll his eyes. "Did I mention you look fantastic?"

"You might have, yes."

"If you're not sure, then it's time I said it again. The wow factor is huge. You look terrific. Seriously."

She laughed, a full laugh filled with delight. "Thank you. You look pretty dapper yourself."

He smiled, happier than he'd been in a long time. He felt like the lunch had gone well. Hopefully it was an omen of great things to come.

He was not disappointed.

Chapter Fourteen

KAYA DRESSED IN SOMETHING NICE, but less fancy, and was back at the gallery by nine o'clock the next morning. She was tired from a late night at the gallery the day before. She didn't know if there would be actual sales that day, but Jonah had asked her to come in and help him out in the morning anyway.

She had a couple of clients who would be at her place for their weekly appointments that afternoon, but at least she could help him get everything back in order, shift some of the items to fill empty spaces, and crate up a few items that they would be shipping to customer's homes after the holidays. Sales had been good—not astounding, but much better than either of them had expected and Jonah had a lot of work ahead of him to pack them up safely.

After the bustle of people the previous night, the gallery seemed a little too empty when Kaya arrived. Jonah had already unlocked the front door, so she was able to walk in and look up the sweeping staircase to the second floor, noting the blank spaces on the wall up the stairs, a couple of statue bases that no longer held anything, and a number of light blue tags that denoted pictures that had been paid for, though the piece was still on display.

"You've moved a lot of things." She found him in the back of the display area.

"As soon as we get the sales packed, I'll frame up the last couple of paintings I have back here and see what I can do about filling out my inventory some more." Jonah looked so pleased, like he couldn't believe his dreams had come true.

"It's not a bad start to the season."

"No, it's not. Manuel is going to be very pleased when he gets his check. Corra is beyond thrilled to have sold six pieces already. We talked for nearly an hour last night. She's already working on something new." Jonah led Kaya back to the storage room. Every flat surface held a piece of art for packaging. He started to show her how to wrap the frames in preparation for crating, but the bell over the door rang.

"I'll get that," Kaya told him. "You focus on things back here. I'll call if I need help." Really, though, Jonah had talked so much about the pieces as they had set up, that she knew a lot about them and the artists.

She helped an older couple, who were in town celebrating their fortieth anniversary, select a pair of similarly-themed western paintings—the last two Manuel had for sale—and Jonah helped her package them up to be taken back to their cabin immediately. Then a trio of forty-something women came in looking for Christmas gifts. Jonah loaded two items into their car nearly an hour later.

A few people came in to look, but didn't purchase anything. Then a tall, nice-looking man in his thirties walked in and asked about the price of the statue in the window of a little girl reaching out to touch a butterfly.

By the time Kaya had to leave to get home for her therapy sessions, they had sold nine more items and Jonah was muttering about needing regular help.

Kaya shrugged into her coat. "I wish I could stay longer. I can tell you need a hand here still."

He stopped in front of her and tugged the lapels of her coat together. "You have a business to run, too. I appreciate you coming in. I might stay open a little later than usual tonight if things are steady. It is the last Saturday to shop before Christmas."

"True." She hadn't realized just how loaded the tourists were in the area, though. She knew rich vacationers kept their community running, but she hadn't paid much attention before. It wasn't like the gallery'd had time to create a reputation—he'd been open less than twenty-four hours. "Do you want me in on Monday?"

"If you can. I'd appreciate it. Even if it's slow for the rest of the week-end, I might not get through everything that needs to be done by Monday night at this rate." He set a hand on her shoulder and leaned in, brushing a brief kiss on her lips. "I could never have gotten to this point without you. Thanks."

She took his hand and gave it a squeeze. "Will I see you in church tomorrow?"

"With any luck." He released her and returned to the back room. She shifted her purse up on her shoulder and went out to her car.

Working at the gallery was exhausting. She appreciated the work, especially right now when things were uncertain in her own life, and she'd loved getting to know Jonah and really understanding what made him tick, but she looked forward to getting back to normal after the holidays.

She missed being able to spend more time with her horses; and she had plenty to take care of on the farm.

At the same time, part-time work might be okay. It would give her a financial cushion, and more time to spend with Jonah. Right now she craved his time and presence almost as much as she did her horses. She was afraid she was sliding dangerously close to full-blown love. He treated their relationship as little more than a convenience. Or maybe he thought more of it than that, but just didn't say so. She told herself to chill—they'd only had one date.

On the way home, Kaya saw cars lined up at the memorial hall. A big poster out front proclaimed the high school art show was that day, but the few people who were outside didn't look happy.

She flipped on the radio, and when it switched from music to a talk program, she changed to a local station for more holiday music. She was practically addicted to holiday music at this time of year. She caught the end of "Rockin' Around the Christmas Tree" and then an advertisement came on. Then the DJ briefed his listeners about what was going on in Echo Ridge for the next few days.

"Now hold onto your hats, everyone. Or should I say, hold onto your paint brushes. The big art show put on by area youth that was supposed to take place today in the Memorial Hall has been postponed because of frozen pipes. The annual school art show is the biggest of the year and the winner earns a scholarship from the Kenworth trust. There's no news of when or where this event will now take place, but we'll post it on our website and Facebook page when they have more information. Stay tuned. And now, well go back to Mike who is at the Bazaar at the Big Barn Boutique talking to Keira Kenworth about what they're doing today."

Kaya listened to a few minutes of chatter about the boutique and how it was being used to not only help vendors in the community, but the less fortunate as well. They cut back to the DJ, who put on the old classic, "Pinecones and Holly Berries." It reminded Kaya of home when she was young and her dad had still been alive. She sang along with it, as she covered the two miles to her house. Bummer about the art show. Hopefully they could get things settled at Memorial Hall quickly.

Chapter Fifteen

SUNDAY MORNING THE PASTOR SPOKE of the true meaning of Christmas and encouraged everyone to be generous in helping their less-fortunate neighbors. The organ music swelled to fill the room, the acoustics making a thrill of appreciation run up Kaya's back. The choir rose from their stand, highlighted by a splash of color from the sun beaming down through the stained glass windows.

After the closing prayer, the congregants frequently stayed to talk, catch up on each other's lives, and share a cup of coffee. This is where she caught up with Reese from the Candy Counter at Kenworth's.

"Hey, how are things going? I heard you quit at Kenworth's," Reese greeted her.

Kaya grimaced. "Yeah, I had to. Cecilia changed my schedule to all of my blackout times and days. I'm working over at the gallery now."

Reese nodded. "I heard that. How is that going?"

"Great. We got everything up and running in time for the opening this week. Jonah's been busy since opening the doors Friday afternoon. Earlier, actually. He sold a piece that was in the window displays over the phone before we opened."

Reese's eyes widened. "That's amazing. I'm so glad to hear it."

"How are things at Kenworth's?" Kaya hadn't had time to go in for the last of her Christmas shopping, but she ought to make some time now that the gallery was functional. Christmas was only days away.

Reese let out a half laugh. "Cecilia is gone."

Kaya wasn't sure if she understood right. "On another one of her buying jaunts, or whatever it was she did?" The woman was apparently gone a lot.

"No, like, gone forever. She went to New York to deal with some promotion, I guess. And she took a job while she was there. She just called up and quit. It was so crazy!" She snapped her fingers. "Hey, I bet they would hire you back on if he doesn't need you at the gallery anymore."

Kaya had liked working the perfume and makeup counters at Kenworth's. It had been a fun change and given her plenty of time to check out the new scents and learn about the newest products—not that she bought much.

On the other hand, she was really enjoying working with Jonah. There was no way she could abandon him. Not until he could get someone else hired. And she needed to get back to her own business full time. "I'm glad Cecilia's gone—seriously, the woman was a menace—but I'm fine where I am. I need to be cutting back my hours some anyway, and getting back to my horses full time."

"Yeah? You sure that's why you won't come back?" Reese seemed a little skeptical of her reasons. "I've seen Jonah Owens. He's hot." Her eyebrows wiggled. A tiny blond woman joined them and Reese asked, "Have you met Natalie? She's the art teacher at the high school."

"I've seen you around," Kaya said in greeting. "I've heard your name before; it's good to have a face to put with it. I'm Kaya Fiedler. I'm currently working at the new gallery."

"Oh yes, I've been meaning to go by and see it now that school is out for the holidays. I met Jonah once."

"He's such a great guy, really." Much better than she had thought after they'd seen each other in Kenworth's. She shouldn't have been surprised, he was Ora's grandson, and he was here to take care of his grandmother. What man does that and is still a jerk? "He's totally gone all-in with the gallery. I'm glad it's working out for him."

"I wish the high school art show had gone as well as the gallery opening." Natalie frowned.

"I heard it had to be postponed. What happened?" Kaya grabbed three cups from the stack and poured each of them a cup of coffee while Reese explained.

"One of the pipes froze and burst. Everything looked fine when they finished setting up Friday night, but when they arrived on Saturday morning, the floor was two inches deep in water. They had to pull the whole thing down and find somewhere else to hold it. The pastor offered the church, but there are so many other things going on here, plus the school is hesitant to hold a school art show in a church, regardless of extenuating circumstances." Natalie pursed her lips. "I wish they could find somewhere else."

Kaya thought of the half-empty walls and pedestals at the gallery. Was it possible that Jonah would consider hosting the school display? "How many entries did the high school show have?"

"I'm not sure exactly. Over fifty," Natalie said.

"Oh," Kaya considered whether they could actually fit that many new items, and how they would have to juggle to make it happen. "That's not a small space."

"It's not a very big space, but not tiny, either. And we need enough room for people to mingle. We'd use the gym, but between school dances, holiday performances, basketball practices and games and whatever else, we can't get in long enough to set up and do the display."

"My brother is so disappointed—he was counting on this for his college applications." Reese stirred in the cream and sugar.

"What kind of displays do they have?" Kaya listened while Natalie listed the number of sculptures versus canvases, or other kinds of displays. It might be possible. Maybe. When Natalie finished, Kaya nodded. "I should take off, but if I think of anywhere that will work for the art show, I'll let you know."

She crossed to the parking lot and got into her truck. Maybe she needed to swing by the gallery on her way home. The space would be tight. Could she even get Jonah to agree? It would bring extra people through the gallery, but it would be a lot of work to set up.

She stopped at Fay's Café and picked up a cup of hot cocoa, then carried it over to the gallery. If she was going to ask something like this of Jonah, a little sweetening up wouldn't go amiss.

The bell rang over the door when she walked in. The room was more than half empty, she'd guess. They'd have to cram things together, but surely they could make it work. She found him wrapping up the last group of sold items, which they had set aside the previous afternoon.

His face brightened when he saw her. "Hey, I didn't expect you to come in today. You can't stay away from this place?"

"I brought you something to drink. I noticed you ducked out right after services." She passed over the cocoa.

He smelled it, grinning. "You do know how to brighten a man's day." His glance flashed down her and back to her face again, taking in the dress she'd worn to church. "And I'm not just talking about the cocoa."

"Thanks. I ordered extra whipped cream. I know how you like it."

"Thank *you*." He took a sip and made yummy noises. "I was flagging. I looked for you to sit with you at church, but I was late and you were hemmed in by the Bradleys. I had to get back here to open shop. So what news did you pick up after church?"

Though she was a little nervous about broaching the subject, she thought she should come out with it. "Did you hear about the pipe breaking and flooding out the high school art show yesterday?"

"Yeah, I picked it up on the radio last night. Have they found a new home for the exhibit yet?"

"No." She took another sip of her dwindling coffee. "I wondered what you'd think of holding it here. It would be a great experience for the kids. The teacher can arrange help to set up the display, since school is out. You were going to be closed on Mondays, so the hustle and bustle won't interfere with your sales. This could bring a lot more locals into your gallery to see what you've got left on display. And then the kids can say their work was displayed in a real art gallery, which won't hurt college admissions for those who are going into art."

Jonah stirred his drink with the hot drink straws and looked up at the corner of the room, his brow crinkling in thought. Then he set down the drink and walked back into the gallery proper. "What can you tell me about the exhibit types and amounts?"

Kaya felt relief as she relayed the information she'd gotten from Natalie. "It would be snug, but I think we could manage it, with the overflow space upstairs."

They hadn't used the space upstairs much the previous week because though he had showed her where he'd planned for a vacuum tube elevator, it hadn't been installed yet, so it wasn't handicapped accessible.

He nodded. "I could shift a few of our more delicate items there, then move the rest of these things over to that side." He gestured to the right as he looked toward the front windows. "We could start with the best pieces near the window to draw people in. It might be a bit snug, but I think we can work it out. If it was only up for a couple of days. What kind of deadline do they have for getting the display available for people to look at?"

Kaya couldn't believe her ears. He was really going to go for it. "Seriously? Thank you!"

She threw her arms around him and hugged him close. Planting a big kiss on his mouth. "I can find out. Let me make a call."

"Just a minute." He reeled her back in again, dragging this kiss out for a long moment. "Thank you for thinking of me. I think the kids deserve nothing less than the best, don't you?"

"Um, yes." A little disoriented from the kiss, Kaya fumbled with her cell phone, and picked up the phone book under the cash register in the back of the gallery. In a few minutes, she had found the art teacher's number and dialed. After filling her in, she passed the phone to Jonah so they could make arrangements.

She couldn't believe it. She couldn't imagine how much work was ahead of them.

Chapter Sixteen

ONCE JONAH GOT OFF THE PHONE with the high school art teacher, he was geared up to make room for the kids. Excitement raced through him, anticipation not unlike when he had been preparing for his opening gala. He grabbed a pad of sticky notes and walked through the gallery, sticking a blank note by each of the pieces that he would display upstairs. They would do only smaller items for now, things that he could photograph and carry down if someone couldn't go up to see them. He'd worry about cataloging them later. And updating his website. That could wait until after Christmas. It wasn't like anyone who hadn't been in the gallery already had the address yet.

"What are you doing?" Kaya stood by the cash register computer, her coffee held at waist height as she watched him move around the room.

"Just marking which works we'll take upstairs to make room for the kids' projects."

He'd already gotten approval for the elevator, and set aside part of the money, but he hadn't wanted to order it until he was sure he would have the cash flow—he still had his grandma's house to make payments on. His mind was moving a hundred miles per minute. "You want to help me move things out of the way, or are you taking your day off and enjoying it, now that you've caused me a lot of extra work?" He smiled, wanting to make sure she knew that he wasn't upset—he thought it was a great idea, it just wasn't the most convenient time to set this up.

A slow smile spread over her mouth. It was a great mouth. "I could probably spare an hour or so."

"Good. I'll have a gallery full of kids first thing tomorrow, so making sure I have room for everything is a must. It's a good thing you already agreed to come in tomorrow."

He'd made a round of the main floor of the gallery, then looked around the room and added a couple more tags to some pottery. Best not to tempt fate. If the pieces were upstairs, away from the high school exhibit, hopefully they wouldn't run the risk of being bumped. "All right. I think that's everything. I'll make adjustments when I see what all they bring in tomorrow."

Kaya drained her cup, then tossed it into the garbage can. "Don't forget your hot cocoa," she said, gripping both sides of a tagged painting's frame. "Let's get this done."

Jonah turned up the radio a couple of notches so they could enjoy the Christmas music into the loft. As the Vienna Boys Choir started singing something in Italian, he hummed along. An hour with Kaya wasn't a bad trade-off for the extra work. He was definitely willing to take less if necessary.

He was careful of her Sunday clothes, but they got most of the items that were going upstairs moved before Kaya took off for a late lunch, and then he had to arrange things on the main floor.

He hummed to the music as he shifted things around, helped a few customers, and packaged up more of the items that had been purchased the previous week. He had several interested customers come in while he worked, and he sold a couple more pieces as well.

Somewhere in there he took a few minutes to run next door to pick up lunch.

He couldn't wait for the next day.

Kaya showed up to work Monday morning wondering how things would go. She knew the teacher was supposed to marshal forces to bring over all of the entries for the high school art show soon. From what she could see, a few things had already been delivered

She stopped on the front walk and looked at the outside of the building. The front display held a bronze statue on one side, and a mixed-media depiction of the Mona Lisa on the other. A huge poster board hung in the window announcing that the art show would open to the public at eleven the next morning and run through Wednesday.

She knocked on the front door when she realized it wasn't open yet, and waved when Jonah stuck his head out to see who was there. He glanced at his watch and shook his head slightly as he crossed the room to her. "Hi, I didn't realize it was so late." He let her in and flipped the sign from closed to open. He took her hand and pulled her toward the back room.

"That's no problem. It looks like you're ready for everyone to arrive." Not that she could see much with the way he was rushing her through the room. He pulled her out of sight of the front windows and into his arms.

"Thanks, we have a lot of work ahead of us, but first…" He kissed her. One hand lifted to her face, brushing back the hair over her ear, his fingers trailing down and around the back of her ear to cup her jaw and tip her face up for a better angle.

Kaya couldn't argue with his version of hello, so she wrapped her arms around his neck and went up on tiptoe for more. She loved kissing this man. She loved the man.

He eventually pulled back. "How are you this morning?"

"Good. Better now than I was a few minutes ago. I can see you're doing well."

"I really am." With a look of regret, he disentangled himself. "We should finish getting the last of the things settled before everyone shows up to set up the high school show."

Kaya removed her coat and passed it to him to hang up, then walked into the gallery again. "Looks like you got most everything moved yesterday."

Kaya was excited that he was so excited about everything. She was glad she had asked him about hosting the show. "Not that I'm not happy, but why are you doing this? I mean, it's been a lot of extra work for you, and potentially very little extra income. If any."

He directed her to help him shift a statue out of the way. "When I was growing up, my dad told me that art was a waste of time, that I'd never make a living at it and ought to give up. If it hadn't been for my art teacher pushing me to pursue the thing I loved, I might not have. I might have just painted a little on the side and been stuck in a job I needed instead of going after my dreams. It was a high school show, not much different than this will be, that really proved to me that I had a chance, that I had a future."

Kaya stopped, waiting until he looked back at her, wanting him to see her eyes when she responded. When he looked at her, a little embar-rassment showing in the set of his mouth, she said, "I think you're pretty amazing, and I don't just mean your art. You, all the way around."

"When I'm not being a gruff jerk, you mean?"

She smiled, remembering that first day. "Yeah, when you're not being a jerk, but I never see that guy anymore. I think he was just frustrated and upset. I can understand that."

"Thanks."

She let that hang in the air for a couple of seconds before changing the subject—she didn't want to choke up in front of him. "How much farther do you want me to shift this?"

He smiled and they got back to work.

The students and a bunch of parents, along with Reese, swarmed the place a few minutes later, carrying in displays and art alike.

"I can't believe this." Reese took in the chaos around them. "Clark is so excited that the show is going to be in a real art gallery. Jonah must be pretty great."

"He is." Kaya looked over and saw him talking with a couple of students, smiling and laughing. "He's excited to be able to give them this opportunity."

"I'd hold onto that one if you can." Reese shot her a knowing look before heading over to join her brother.

"Oh, I plan on it." Kaya basked in the warmth that radiated through her every time she thought of Jonah Owens.

Natalie and Jonah had already discussed the layout and went to work directing traffic and giving orders. It was amazing, seeing the whole project come together. Kaya helped wherever they needed her and answered the phone half a dozen times in the next two hours, then, after the students had left, watched Natalie put tags on the winning pieces.

She knew when everyone arrived the next morning for the show, there would be a lot of excited teens.

Chapter Seventeen

JONAH RANG UP ANOTHER SALE that evening and offered to carry the purchase out to the man's car, but the customer, John Dolinger, said he'd take it himself. Jonah held the door for him, then turned to greet Evelyn, Shyanne and Chad who were walking into the gallery. "It's great to see you here. I'm so glad you could come." He shook all three hands, making the children grin at being treated like adults.

"Thanks, we decided we needed a night out, and since we heard on the radio that you're hosting the high school show, we decided to make the trip up to see your gallery." Evelyn looked around, pleasure in her expression. "I bet it was fancy on Thursday night for the grand opening."

"I froze the extra refreshments, if you guys would like some after you look around." Jonah genuinely liked the kids, and he felt empathy for the single mom, trying to handle two disabled children on her own. It had to be difficult. "I have a surprise for you, too."

"You do?" Evelyn's brows lifted.

Chad practically vibrated with anticipation, "Do you have a surprise for me, too?"

"It's for all of you." He hoped it was a good surprise as he led them back to where he had hung the depictions of Evelyn's kids.

"Is that me?" Shyanne stared at her face on the watercolor. "It's not, right? She's way too pretty."

"It's absolutely you, and I think I should have tried again. She's not nearly as pretty as you are." Jonah gave her a quick pat on the shoulder.

"It says it's on hold." Chad looked at him. "The picture of me is on hold." He stared at the drawing, his brow furrowing.

"They both are. I wanted to make sure you got to see them. You want to know a secret?"

"Yeah, what is it?" Chad was not using a quiet voice, by any means, but Jonah wasn't worried about it.

"I haven't been able to paint for a long time. Over a year, but then I saw you guys, and you're both so special and so excited about Kaya's animals, and I just had to draw and paint again. I couldn't help it. It's like you're my muses."

"Your amuses?" Chad asked.

"His muse, like his inspiration," Shyanne said with an air of hauteur. "That's really cool. Mom, can you buy them? I want it so much. There I am with Morning Star. She's so pretty."

He'd had to go onto Kaya's website to get a picture of the goat, or he wouldn't have managed to get the drawing right. As it was, he'd had to remember Shyanne from memory, and the image wasn't nearly as good as if he'd had a photo to work off of. Chad was only marginally recognizable, which was part of the reason he had drawn him partially in silhouette. "They aren't as true to your kids as I would have liked, but I only met them twice," he said to Evelyn.

"I think they're still remarkable." She sniffed softly, then waved her hands at the children. "Go look around at everything. Don't touch anything, and don't goof off."

"Yes, Mom," Shyanne said, and wheeled off. Chad had to be told a second time, before he ambled off.

"He's going to be dead bored in three minutes, isn't he?" Jonah asked.

"Yep. I brought a graphic novel for him." Evelyn patted her large, red purse. "The paintings really are fantastic. I would love to buy them, but unless I get a job, even part-time, I don't know if that will happen."

He had wondered how that was going. "What about the house?"

Tears formed in her eyes. "I need to work if I'm going to get a mortgage. I've had so many problems finding anything that will work around their school schedules and appointments. I love that house, Jonah, I just don't know if I can do it." She rubbed a knuckle under her right eye, catching a tear. "Unless you're hiring." She let out a soft chuckle.

Jonah stared at her for a moment. "Do you have a background in art? How about retail?"

"Retail, yes. And some business classes. Before Shyanne was born I actually was assistant manager at a dress shop. I don't know a huge amount about art, but it looks like you have quite an eclectic collection, and I'm not talking about the high school stuff."

Jonah weighed his options and gave himself a few second to see how he felt about it. "Have you done any bookkeeping?"

"A lot, actually."

"How much do you have to earn in order to qualify for the loan?"

"About seven hundred a month."

Jonah quickly did the math. He could manage to hire her for fifteen hours most weeks, especially if he was going to be painting again. "How about if we start you at thirteen an hour. That's about fifteen hours per week. We can flex around your kid's schedules starting when they go back to school after the holidays."

Her eyes went wide. "Are you serious?"

"Yeah. I am. I have a good feeling about you and your kids. And I know my gram would like you. She might want to meet you first, if you don't mind going by to meet with her tonight. She's in a rehab center after breaking her hip."

Evelyn smiled so brightly, she outshone the light on the paintings of her children. "Do you think I could work off the cost of the paintings?"

"The one of Shyanne becomes yours as soon as you sign on the contract, even if things fall through and you don't buy the house. Consider it a signing bonus. I can work something out with you for Chad's." He quoted a price and terms and she agreed, happily.

Jonah called his grandma to set up the visit. It seemed most everything was working out after all.

Chapter Eighteen

THE HIGH SCHOOL SHOW WAS DONE and over Wednesday night, and Jonah was pleased with how it went. He'd spoken to the two top high school artists about distributing their winning art as prints, both were enthusiastic about the prospect. Reese's brother Clark was one of them, which had pleased Kaya, giving Jonah even more satisfaction.

Most of the high school pieces were gone by the time they closed the doors. The teacher said she'd swing by for the rest the next day.

He'd had a lot of people come through who hadn't realized the gallery had opened yet, despite his best efforts at publicity the previous week. He had agreed to host the exhibit for the kids, but the side benefit for the business wasn't bad. He'd even sold a few pieces because of the exhibit.

Everything finished up by seven that night, and he locked up, heading to the back room for the package he had wrapped early that morning and exited out the back door.

Jonah arrived at Kaya's to see the barn lights still shining, with only the porch and driveway lights on at the house. There were no strange vehicles in the back drive, so her last clients must have been gone. His stomach jumped like disturbed grasshoppers and his palms felt a little clammy, despite the cold. He grabbed the large package and went to the front door, leaving it on the covered front porch.

Going around to the barn, he could hear the goats bleating. He opened the door to find Kaya stroking the muzzle on one of the horses, talking to it in low tones. Jonah couldn't understand the words, but he understood the love. How had he not seen that from the beginning, the way she loved and cared for them, how important the animals were to her? Sasha, the enormous white dog, walked over to greet him. He cleared his throat to alert Kaya to his presence.

Kaya didn't jump or show any surprise at his appearance. "Hi, I wondered if it was you."

His brow lowered in surprise. "You knew I was here?"

"Sasha alerted me a minute ago, but she didn't seem nervous, so I knew she knew who it was. She's very quick to learn the sound of people's vehicles."

She crossed the barn to him. "I didn't expect to see you tonight."

"I didn't expect to come. I was going to wait a couple of days, but then I just couldn't."

Her lips curved up as she slid her hands around his waist. "That sounds promising." She wore her coveralls, insulated to keep her warm since the temperatures had plummeted again. She was still beautiful, no matter what she wore.

"Do you need any help out here?" He wanted to make sure he had her undivided attention when they went inside.

"No, I'm done. I was just telling everyone goodnight."

His arms went around her shoulder, pulling her closer, enjoying the unhurried moment. "Is that something you do every night, come say good night to them?"

"Absolutely. The chickens just get a group greeting, though, I generally count heads and call it good. They're already sleeping when my sessions end."

"That's how it goes sometimes. I'm sure Belle appreciates not being disturbed."

Kaya nodded. "I'm sure she does."

He leaned in and kissed her, their lips meeting softly at first, lingering, testing. He dragged the moment out, enjoying himself before stepping back and taking her hand. They headed for the outside door, pausing while she flipped off all but the outside motion-sensing lights. Sasha joined them outside the barn, set to do her job of protecting everyone for the night.

Jonah gave her head an extra rub before he and Kaya entered through the back door of the house.

"Would you like some cocoa and gingerbread cupcakes? I need to clean up for bed soon, but I can sit with you for a while and take some time to unwind."

The anxious excitement that had been percolating inside him since deciding to come increased as he headed for the front. "I left something on the porch."

When he came back, she was already putting milk in a double-boiler. "What's that?"

"It's for you. I've been working on it for a few days now."

Kaya's face brightened. "Is it one of yours? I'd love to have one of your paintings."

He hoped she felt the same way about the rest of the things he wanted to say. He took the seat she gestured him to at the table while she brought over the ceramic mugs and cocoa mix, along with a half-empty bag of mini marshmallows. She set a few cupcakes in a bakery box from Fay's Café. "Do you have cocoa a lot?" It was a nice thing to have in common.

"It's a good way to warm up after working outside, especially since it's too late to have coffee when I have to be up so early."

They shared small talk while they prepared their cups and poured the hot milk when it was ready.

Jonah took a sip of the creamy mix. He was surprised at how great the goats' milk was in the cocoa. "This is terrific."

"Surprised?"

"I thought it would taste funny because of the goat's milk."

"Depends on the goats, mostly. The right breeds just taste like milk." She shot him a wink.

"Right. I guess that makes sense." He was stalling for time. They'd never talked about what they were or where they were going. He worried he was rushing things, but at the same time, he couldn't put it off any longer. He just had no idea where to start.

As usual, she made it easy for him. "So what's in the package? Obviously it's framed."

"Go ahead and open it. I know it's a couple days early." That was a good place to start. Wasn't it why he'd brought it?

"You're not going to make me wait until Christmas?"

"No, I couldn't take the waiting." They shared a smile over their mugs. He set his down and pushed the painting toward her. "Go ahead."

Kaya put down her own mug and lifted the package to the table beside her. She paused for a couple of seconds, as if letting the anticipation build, then tore a big piece of the paper away, revealing a painting of herself on the ice at Chickadee Lake. She was suffused in the soft glow of a nearby pine tree, which had been strung with colored lights, and a light from somewhere nearby, silhouetted her against the night sky. She looked happy and bright and beautiful, just the way he thought of her. Kaya ripped back the rest of the paper, so she could see the entire thing.

She stared at the painting for a long moment. Prolonging his agony of wondering what she thought.

"Say something or I'm going to have a heart attack," Jonah finally broke the silence.

"Wow. Seriously, this is so beautiful. I can't believe you painted me. It's fantastic. And very, very flattering. I know I didn't look half that good." She didn't take her eyes off of it. Her fingers traced over the thin plaque at the bottom. It read *One Winter's Night*.

She liked it. Jonah didn't know why that was such a relief. She'd liked the other paintings he'd done, but this one mattered more.

When Kaya looked up at him, there were tears glistening in her eyes. "I can't imagine a more perfect gift. Thank you."

"No, thank you." He took her hand, studying every nuance of

her expression. "I thought painting was behind me. Honestly, it's been so long, and I just hadn't even felt like picking up a brush in over a year. I'd tried a few times, but I never got that rush, that inner demand to do it until now. I know that's all you."

"No it's not, it was just time—"

He couldn't let her think that. "No, it really wasn't. It was you. I thought after Janet that relationships just weren't worth it. I couldn't stand to be in that kind of pain again, but looking back, what we had was worth it even though it hurt when I lost her. And I know that what you and I have is worth the risk. I know we haven't really known each other long. I know I haven't always been great to deal with, but I haven't felt this way... ever."

The tears were streaming down her cheeks now and he worried they didn't mean what he hoped they meant. She didn't speak for a long moment, so long he couldn't stand the quiet any longer.

"I know you deserve poetry and beautiful words, but I'm not good with words, I'm good with paint, so I hoped it would speak for me. The fact is, I love you. I'm in love with you. I didn't expect it, but I knew it that night, on the ice, and the feeling has grown every moment I've spent with you. I'll understand if you don't feel the same way."

Kaya put her finger over his lips, making him stop. She sucked in a ragged breath and finally spoke. "Your painting spoke volumes, and your words are practically poetry on their own. I love you too. I love how you take good care of your grandma, and how you gave a struggling mother a job so she can buy a house that will make her life easier."

He broke in, "A house I was selling, so that wasn't exactly selfless."

"Shush." She paused just long enough to be sure he wasn't going to interrupt again, then plunged on. "I love how important art is to you, and how you've gone out of your way to help new, struggling artists. I spoke with Corra for quite a while about how you helped her out. I love that you paused, even though you were busy and were tight on funds, to buy gifts for a couple of children from the Hope Tree. And that even though you probably didn't want to see my face after the chicken at the rehab center, you hired me anyway."

He shrugged, actually feeling embarrassed. "I was desperate."

Kaya huffed and gave him the stink eye. "And apparently you can't take a compliment."

Jonah laughed and pulled her close, kissing her to end the parade of compliments. Things wouldn't be perfect, but he knew they could make it through anything. "To think I almost turned you away when you came to the door for the job."

"I'm glad you didn't."

"Me too." He kissed her again.

Jay's Gingerbread
Cupcakes

3/4 Cup butter, softened
1 1/2 Cups sugar
3 eggs
3/4 Cup milk
3/4 cup molasses
1 1/2 tsp vanilla
1 Tbsp baking powder
3/4 tsp salt
2 1/2 Cups flour
1 1/2 tsp ginger
3/4 tsp cloves
3/4 tsp cinnamon

Preheat oven to 350 degrees.

Mix the flour, baking powder and spices in a bowl and set aside. Cream the butter, sugar and eggs, in a mixing bowl then mix in the milk, molasses and vanilla. Slowly incorporate the dry ingredients while mixing. Fill cupcake liners half full and bake at 350 degrees for 18-22 minutes. Frost with your favorite vanilla or cinnamon frosting.

You can bake this in a 9x13 instead for a cake. Preheat the oven to 375 and bake for about 25 minutes.

Acknowledgments

This anthology was such a great learning experience for me. I had never written a story that was so closely connected to other stories with so many characters and elements that needed to overlap without infringing. I want to thank Rachelle Christensen, Lucy McConnell, Connie Sokol, and Cami Checketts for letting me be part of the Echo Ridge Anthologies. It has been great to see how our friendships have grown through the experience.

I also want to thank the lovely group of women who helped me edit this story—Diana Shanks, Brooke Heaton, Kayla Batty, and Shelley Carr who helped me catch so many of the elusive typos that dog every author's heels. Thanks to Pauline Buttrey, my amazing assistant who takes care of so many of the details that elude my brain.

And of course a big thanks to my hubby Bill, who puts up with any author idiosyncrasies and loves me all the same.

About Heather Tullis

HEATHER TULLIS has been reading romance for as long as she can remember and has been publishing in the genre since 2009. She has published more than twenty books. When she's not dreaming up new stories to write, or helping out with her community garden, she enjoys playing with her dogs and cat, cake decorating, trying new jewelry designs, inventing new ways to eat chocolate, and hanging out with her husband.

Learn more about her at her website and sign up for her newsletter at http://heathertullis.com/ Instagram at https://www.instagram.com/tullisheather/or her Facebook fan page http://www.facebook.com/HeatherTullisBooks.